FIRST WARNING

Protruding from a low, evergreen hedge were a pair of trousered legs, a man's legs.

The man lay flat on his back. Wide-open eyes stared up at the moonlit sky. He was not anyone Peter could recall having seen before.

Peter bent down, convinced by the staring eyes that the man was dead, though he could see no wound. He reached out to touch the man's neck, to find the jugular pulse with his fingers.

Then he stood up quickly and turned away. The man's mouth gaped open and empty. *Someone had taken the time to cut out his tongue.*

The Peter Styles Mystery Series

THE LARKSPUR CONSPIRACY

A Peter Styles Mystery

by
Judson Philips

PINNACLE BOOKS • NEW YORK CITY

THE LARKSPUR CONSPIRACY

A Pinnacle Book, published by special arrangement with
Dodd, Mead & Company.

ISBN: 0-523-00374-9

First printing, June 1974

Printed in the United States of America

PINNACLE BOOKS, INC.
275 Madison Avenue
New York, N.Y. 10016

PART ONE

The Puzzle

CHAPTER 1

"THERE ARE A thousand women who would be fun in bed,"
Peter Styles said, his voice harsh and a little unsteady, "but
there is only one in the whole world to share my life with
me." He turned away to the windows of Frank Devery's
office and looked down at the lights of the traffic moving
uptown on Madison Avenue. His hands were jammed deep
in the pockets of his tweed jacket, hiding his clenched fists.

"It's not final!" Devery said. He was slumped in his
leather desk chair, chewing on an unlighted cigar. He was a
short, square man, with an aggressive look to him that was
somehow dissolved at this moment by compassion for his
friend.

Peter spun around from the window. "How much more
final can it be?" he asked.

It had come out of the blue, at a time when he was high
on happiness. Grace's letter was in his pocket. "We leave
Bangladesh tomorrow, Peter. I have agreed to stop over in
Saigon for no more than ten days to help set up a civilian
clinic for the hundreds of thousands of displaced people in
that unhappy country. And then, my darling, I will be on

my way home forever. I've had my fill of being a do-gooder, Peter. From now on all I want to be forever is your wife, your love, the other half of you who are the other half of me. In less than three weeks, darling, we'll start to live for ourselves and let the rest of the world take care of itself."

Then, a few hours ago, there had come a phone call from a half-forgotten friend in the State Department.

"I'm sorry to have to bring you bad news, Peter."

"Bad news?" Peter tried to think what could be considered "bad news" in connection with his work as a feature writer for *Newsview* Magazine, the national weekly edited by Frank Devery. He wasn't involved in any research that had to do with the State Department, unless perhaps there was some unsuspected connection with the Larkspur story.

"The plane on which your wife was traveling from Bangladesh to Saigon is missing," the friend said.

And the world turned dark and cold.

"There were four army doctors, two medics, your wife, and the pilot and co-pilot aboard," the friend said. "We lost radio contact with them when they were less than an hour away from Saigon. It's mountainous country. There had been no word from them of any trouble. They—they've just disappeared. 'Copters have been looking for some sign of them for a day. I'm sorry to say there is nothing."

"How do I get out there?" Peter asked, in a voice he didn't recognize. *All I want to be forever is your wife, your love—*

"You don't."

"Come on, Preston!"

"There are still thousands of men missing out there, Peter. If we let one family member go out there we'd be swamped."

4

"So fix it! So keep it quiet but get me there!"

"I'm sorry, Peter. You're not a trained aerial observer. You'd only take the place of a skilled man in a search. You're not a mountain climber."

The friend was remembering Peter's leg, lost in a long-ago violence. He walked without a limp; he played golf and danced. But he was not, God help him, a mountain climber.

"You don't have any special talents for a search of this kind. Before you could get there we will have found them, or—"

"Or not!"

"Let's face it, Peter, the chances of our finding them alive are just about zero."

"Are they zero?"

"Not quite. Not till we know for sure. But I have to tell you there's no place for a B-57 to land in those mountains."

"Parachutes?"

"If they had time. I'm most awfully sorry, friend."

"God damn you!" Peter shouted.

And then it was on the radio and in the evening papers. NINE AMERICANS MISSING ON MERCY FLIGHT. WIFE OF FAMOUS JOURNALIST AMONG THOSE FEARED LOST.

There was only one person Peter could go to who would not give him pity, who wouldn't crack him up with kindness. That person was Frank Devery, his boss, a friend who had seen him through the loss of his leg and helped to bail him out of a sea of self-pity. Devery had been his best man at his wedding to Grace. He knew her, loved her in his fashion, knew what a very special, irreplaceable person she was.

"It's not final," was Devery's message. "So they parachuted. So it could take them weeks to walk out of those

5

goddamn mountains. I flew over them in World War Two."

"Suppose she's badly hurt?"

"She's got four doctors and two medics with her."

"Frank, what in God's name do I do?"

"First you drink a double Jack Daniels," Devery said, pointing to the portable office bar. "Second, you remember —and nobody should remember better than you—that when the world caves in on you, you work! You work till you're exhausted with it and you keep on after that. You've got this Larkspur story to investigate and finish. Have you forgotten that the first installment of it is out on ·the stands today? Would you believe it if I told you our switchboard has been swamped with calls from people who want to know the whole truth? You started it and you bloody well are going to finish it."

"Oh, Christ, Frank, do you know what you're asking?"

"Sure I do. But what else, chum? You go home and cry yourself to sleep? I had all the self-pity I needed from you seven or eight years ago. You can't help Grace. You can only keep yourself in one piece in case she gets lucky and walks out of there."

Peter poured himself a drink, swallowed it, and put the glass down hard on Devery's desk. A tiny smile twitched at the corner of his mouth. His eyes seemed sunk in their. sockets. "I know you, you bastard," he said. "The minute I walk out of here you'll cry for her."

"So that's my business," Devery said. "Your business is to stay in one piece, keep working, and speak to God about it if you're in contact with him."

Peter looked away. "It's cold in those mountains," he said.

"It's cold just about everywhere in this bloody world," Devery said. "You're on the trail of about as cold a business in this Larkspur conspiracy as you're likely to come across in a lifetime. You going to let thousands of people down while you indulge in being sorry for yourself?"

It was not cold, weatherwise, in New York that August evening. Peter decided to walk from the *Newsview* offices on Fifty-second Street to his apartment on Irving Place. The exercise might relax muscles that ached from tension.

Sometimes when you walked the city streets the people you passed seemed like neighbors, brothers; sometimes they seemed furtive, sinister strangers; sometimes aggressive and hostile enemies. Peter guessed it really depended on your own state of mind how they appeared. Tonight it was a world of enemies.

Devery hadn't referred to it, but he had known very well that what he called the Larkspur Conspiracy had an indirect connection with Grace. A few summers ago Grace had only been a dream in Peter's life. She was the widow of a friend of Peter's who had been shot down by some crackpot in a protest march. Grace and her husband had been working in the Peace Corps in Africa, and when they came back to this country Steve Minafee had been murdered. Peter had helped solve the crime, and had fallen in love with a woman who was grieving over her own loss. It would never work for him, he knew. But a couple of years later during a hot summer, hot racially, Peter had come across Grace working in a welfare clinic in Harlem. Her wounds were healed and his dream came true. During that summer when New York City seemed to be poised on top of a time bomb, Grace had introduced him to a strange man in the black community named Nathan Hale Jones. Jones was a cultured, highly educated man, a revolutionary at heart, a realist in action. He was tall, slim, with a Fu Manchu mustache and beard, wearing black glasses day and night that hid his eyes—and his inner thoughts—from any-one in communication with him. This was a man who knew all the secrets of the black community, all the hatreds, all the fears, all the injustices. He was an enemy to fear, a friend to cherish. He trusted almost no white people, but Grace was a kind of heroine in Nathan Jones's book. Be-cause Peter was Grace's man, Nathan Jones had come to him for help about a month ago.

Nathan Jones didn't move in the city without protection. He appeared at Peter's Irving Place apartment one night, flanked by two giant bodyguards. Peter was glad to see him; glad because he was a friend of Grace's.

A little later he was glad to see Nathan as a reporter and journalist, because Nathan had a story. The two body-guards had been dispatched to the little garden at the rear of Peter's ground-floor apartment. They had refused drinks, accepted coffee. Nathan Jones, black glasses hiding his feelings, asked politely about Grace and learned that she was in Bangladesh, heading up a rescue mission. He learned it from Peter and had obviously known all about it before-hand. He was a polite man. He let you talk and Peter liked to talk about Grace, *the other half of him*—

"But you didn't come here to talk about Grace, Nathan."

The black man lit a thin, black cigar. For a moment twin flames from his lighter were reflected in the opaque black glasses.

"Ever hear of the Larkspur Project, Styles?" Nathan had never called Peter by his first name.

"It's a big, low-cost housing project in your part of the city."

"Maybe."

"How do you mean 'maybe'? They've broken ground, haven't they?"

"Maybe."

8

"Tell me whatever you want to tell me, Nathan, or don't tell me if you've changed your mind. You've come here as Grace's friend. You can count on my keeping a confidence."

"I know that or I wouldn't be here," Nathan said. He looked at the ash on the end of his thin cigar. "Big to-do over Larkspur. First time in history that private capital has invested in public housing on this scale. No city help, no state help, no federal help. A big-hearted investment banker named Walter Girard dreamed it up. Very rich man in his fifties, married to a very glamorous second wife who is a musical comedy star. Elaine Summers. Heard of her?"

"Of course. She's playing in something right now called *Glamor Town*."

"A doll," Nathan said, dryly, "if you like white dolls. Girard got some rich friends of his to put up the first money and then he went out into the community, particularly my community—the black community—to raise the rest of what was needed. Little people put up more than they could afford, thousands of them. It meant a decent place to live for many of them—a place without filth; a place without roaches or rats; a place with plumbing and hot water and paint. Everybody was full of love for everybody. White men and black men were brothers. Oh man!"

"Love or not they made it," Peter said.

Nathan nodded. Smoke curled up around that black, Fu Manchu face. "Six months ago Walter Girard, chairman of the fund-raising drive, announced they'd made it. Thirty-seven million dollars!"

"Wow!"

"The land was bought for the modest sum of three hundred thousand." Nathan's voice was bitter. "Black owners. The price was low. One of the best white architectural firms in the city drew the plans and eventually the

9

exact specifications. They were approved. There were two black men on an executive committee of twelve who approved the plans. Contractors made bids, and an Italian firm known as Petrocelli Brothers got the job. White, you'll notice. So Petrocelli Brothers moved in about two months ago to break ground, to start the work. You know anything about building, Styles?"

"Not really."

"What was moved onto the site is a joke. Not enough equipment to put up a prefab bungalow. Two months—they've scratched a little earth."

"So, as usual, there is graft," Peter said.

"Right on!" Nathan said. He fumbled inside the folds of his black linen jacket. What he produced was a very small tape recorder. "Care to listen?"

"Sure."

The tape began to turn.

"Tom?" a man's voice said. "I thought you should know that Girard has arranged for two numbered Swiss bank accounts."

"Great," a second voice said.

"The money will have been transferred in a few days. It will certainly be a few months before anybody begins to smell a rat."

"And then?" the second voice asked.

"Then we proceed as planned."

The tape stopped.

"Who are they?" Peter asked.

"I don't know," Nathan said. "The woods are full of guys named Tom."

"Where did you get it?"

"Let me put it this way," Nathan said. He knocked the ash off his cigar into a brass tray beside his chair. It was an almost elegant gesture. "A friend, who is an expert at

10

electronics, was trying to get something on some gangland characters who have been pushing heroin in Harlem. He tapped a telephone in an office which the alleged gang boss uses as a front in Harlem. Anthony Larch, Insurance Broker. The setup my friend installed taped telephone calls from Larch's phone. Hundreds of them. Some legitimate insurance stuff. Some, if you could read between the lines, had to do with traffic in drugs. And this one. This isolated one that has to do with Walter Girard and Swiss bank accounts."

"Your friend doesn't know to whom the voices belong?"

"No. One of them is named Tom. It's as if someone was in Larch's office on business and just happened to use the phone for something that wasn't business. Whoever it was wasn't playing games, Styles. The conversation was for real."

"The tape can't be used as evidence unless your friend had a court order to bug the telephone," Peter said.

"He didn't have a court order. For some time, Styles, we have been suspicious. The slowness of the work, a dozen other things I can tell you about. Graft as usual. But now— well, now we wonder if this isn't just another big white swindle at the expense of the blacks."

"You've come here because you want me to do something," Peter said.

Nathan nodded. "I can produce a group of small investors in Larkspur. They have tried to ask questions and they've had a polite brushoff from the contractor, from Girard, from the lawyer for the Larkspur Fund. The construction delays are due to material shortages. Pentagon priorities, that sort of excuse. But they have good reason to believe they are being had. This tape, you may guess, has scared the hell out of them. Their money has been spirited out of the country."

11

"You can't use the tape."

"They have heard rumors. They are panicked. Getting nowhere with the brass, they come to you, known as a journalist who crusades for truth and justice. You are convinced that they have heard enough in the rumor market for them to be entitled to reassurance. You put that in print."

"Perhaps, if—"

"You can say in print that they've heard the rumor that a large part of the money has been spirited away into Swiss bank accounts. You don't say it's so. You just say 'it's being said.' You just say that these people are entitled to an accounting, to a reassurance.

Peter was silent for a moment. "You could have made that tape yourself, Nathan, just to suck me in."

"But you know I didn't."

Peter nodded slowly. "Yes, I know you didn't. I'd have to sell Devery, my boss. Can he hear the tape?"

"Sure. Take the machine."

"If anything happens to it—"

"Man, you don't think that's the original tape, do you? There are a hundred conversations on the original that have nothing to do with Larkspur. This is a tape made from a tape."

"I'm not sure I see what good a story will do," Peter said, frowning. "This group of small investors—?"

Nathan's smile was tight-lipped. "Ten-dollar investors, Styles. But for them it was like giving blood."

"The answer will be—"

"—that they are a bunch of superstitious, suspicious, uneducated niggers," Nathan said. "But you mention those Swiss bank accounts and somebody is going to twitch. Let me give all the details, the no work, a dozen other things; the brushoffs. It's enough for you to ask a question that's ignored when these people ask it. You ask it and they'll get an answer that will appear to be satisfactory, but someone is likely to panic. We'll be watching."

"I'll talk to Devery."

"Fine." Nathan stood·up, tall and straight. The two bodyguards appeared from the garden. One of them went out the front door and after a moment returned.

"All clear," he said.

"Give my regards to Grace when she gets back," Nathan said. He smiled. "In case you're feeling noble about helping a black cause, Styles, remember there are hundreds of white investors involved too." He went out, one bodyguard in front of him and one behind.

A week of digging and Peter was convinced that Nathan had reason to suspect. Devery bought it and Peter wrote his story. As he walked down Madison Avenue toward his apartment that night he passed a newsstand. That day's issue of *Newsview* was displayed. LARKSPUR PROJECT QUESTIONED. And beside it a morning paper. NINE AMERICANS MISSING ON MERCY FLIGHT.

It was like a knife thrust in his gut.

He turned east on Twentieth Street and hesitated outside the door of his club, the Players. He was tempted not to stay alone, but if he went in he would be surrounded by friends sympathizing with him. He couldn't stand that either.

He walked slowly around the corner to the building where he lived. He paused by the brass mailboxes. There could be letters for him. There could be a letter from Grace. He wondered if he could bear to look at it, knowing it had been written, full of happiness, before she'd taken off on that fatal flight.

The box was empty.

He let himself into his apartment and switched on the

lights. What he saw froze him in the doorway. The place had been torn apart. Books had been taken out of the bookcases and thrown on the floor. The upholstered armchair and the couch and been ripped open and the stuffing searched. The drawers of his desk had been yanked out and their contents dumped on the floor. Pictures had been taken off the walls and their backings ripped away. A photograph of Grace on his desk had been smashed and her picture lay on the floor, an ugly heel mark on her face. He took a half-paralyzed step to the bedroom. The king-size double bed had been torn apart, the mattress slashed open. His clothes had been taken out of the closet and the linings of his coats cut apart, torn. Rugs had been rolled back and tossed aside. The search, he guessed, had been rapid, handled by more than one person, but he had never seen anything quite so thorough, so total.

He walked, still trance-like, toward the French windows that opened out onto his garden, stepping over books and papers. The front door had been intact. He had to believe that the searchers had come through the maze of back alleys and over the board fence that surrounded the garden. He wondered if they had dug up his flower beds to search for buried treasure.

What the hell had they been looking for? There were paintings of value that had been kicked around and left behind. His first quick survey told him that nothing had been taken, only searched.

He stopped just outside the French windows, his heart jamming hard aginst his ribs. Protruding from behind a low, evergreen hedge, were a pair of trousered legs, a man's legs.

The man lay flat on his back. Wide-open eyes stared up at the moonlit sky. He was black. He was not anyone Peter could recall having seen before.

Peter bent down, convinced by the staring eyes that the man was dead, though he could see no wound. He had to make sure. He reached out to touch the man's neck, to find the jugular pulse with his fingers if it existed.

Then he stood up quickly and turned away. He thought for a moment he was going to vomit. The man's mouth gaped open and empty. Someone had taken the time to cut out his tongue.

CHAPTER 2

PETER STOOD WHERE he was. He could feel himself shaking from head to foot. It came partly from horror and partly from a sudden anger that was so intense he wanted to cry out to ease the pressure. Finally he took a handkerchief out of his pocket and covered the dead man's gaping face with it. No one should have to look at that mutilation unprepared.

In crisis moments you turn to friends if you can. Peter called police headquarters on the phone and asked for Lieutenant Maxvil of Homicide. The Lieutenant was off duty, but Peter had his home phone in the address book beside the phone. Only the book wasn't beside the phone. It had been handled by the intruders, like everything else in the apartment, and then tossed aside. Peter found it under a litter of papers and letters.

Gregory Maxvil was part of a new breed of cops, college educated, scientifically trained, and with a law degree on the side. Peter had met this intense, hard-driving young man during a murder case he'd covered for the magazine. They'd become something more than casual friends. Greg Maxvil was a highly trained detective; he was a man who

16

knew his city from one end to the other, the people in high places, political places, places of influence. You want to know who to talk to about what went on under the surface in city life Greg Maxvil was the man to ask. Only a few nights ago Peter had spent a pleasant drinking time with Maxvil, talking about the Larkspur business.

Maxvil was at home, only a few blocks away.

"Man, I just heard the news about your wife," Maxvil said. "What can I say? There isn't anything to say except something corny, like 'while there's life there's hope.' I'm so sorry, Peter."

"I didn't call you for sympathy," Peter said. His voice sounded so unlike him that Maxvil instantly detected special vibrations.

"What the hell's the matter with you?"

"I just got back to my place five or six minutes ago. It's been torn apart, someone searching for something. In the garden is a dead man I don't know. So I called you."

"You notified the police officially?"

"I called you." ··

"You suspect your dead man was murdered?"

"I don't know what killed him, but someone cut out his tongue."

"Jesus!"

"He's black. I suppose it could be connected with the Larkspur thing we were talking about the other day."

"Sit tight," Maxvil said. "There'll be a patrol car there in a couple of minutes. I'll make it as quick as I can. Peter?"

"Yes."

"Don't touch anything except that phone, and a liquor bottle and glass if you need to."

There was something he had to touch; the photograph of Grace that had been ripped out of its frame and tossed on the floor. He looked at the black heel mark in the middle of

17

her lovely face.

"Sonsofbitches!" he said.

Then he called Devery, who was still at the office. He told him what he'd found. "I'm only guessing, Frank, but I think someone was looking for whatever I might have to back up the story in today's magazine."

"What do you want me to do?"

"I have a number for Nathan Jones." Peter gave Devery the number. "You won't get him, but whoever answers will carry a message to him in a hurry. Have him call you back. Tell him what's happened. This dead man in my garden may mean something to him."

The front doorbell rang.

Peter opened the door to two uniformed cops.

"I'm Sergeant Miller," the first one said. "My partner, patrolman Sikowski. We had a call that you've got trouble here. You Mr. Styles?"

"Come in," Peter said.

The two cops looked around the disordered apartment. Peter led them out into the garden and they stood staring down at the dead man. Peter lifted the handkerchief and he heard both men react.

"What killed him?" Miller asked.

"No visible wounds as he lies there," Peter said. "Except—"

"Christ, who would do a thing like that?" Sikowski asked. He was young and he looked shaken.

"Must have got him in the back," Miller said. "I'll report in. Your phone?"

"Just inside the door."

Miller went inside. Sikowski took a handkerchief out of his pocket and wiped his face with it. "You don't know who he is?"

"Never saw him before," Peter said. He covered the dead

18

face again.

"What did they steal?" Sikowski asked, looking back into the living room.

"Nothing that I can see so far."

Peter turned away. He needed help; help to focus on the moment. It was as if two separate movie films were being run through the projector at the same time. There was the wreckage of the apartment, and there was the vision of a giant plane plummeting to earth, flames blazing at its engines and wings; there was the dead face in the garden, and the dead face of the woman he loved, lying in the twisted, smoking remains of the downed plane; there was the picture of the black man in the garden fighting to save himself from the faceless men in Peter's apartment, and there was a picture of Grace trying to fight her way through dark jungles, surrounded by equally faceless and unidentifiable dangers.

"You didn't take that drink," a voice said at Peter's side. It was Maxvil. Peter hadn't answered his doorbell. This wasn't any longer his home. It was "the scene of the crime."

Peter turned to his friend. He couldn't know how ravaged his face was. Maxvil's dark eyes were narrowed with concern.

"Show me your dead man," he said.

Peter turned toward the flower bed. Maxvil looked, and then bent down and picked up Peter's handkerchief, revealing the mutilated face. Watching him, Peter saw Maxvil's lips move in what he guessed was a soundless profanity.

Maxvil faced Peter, his eyes blazing. "I know him," he said, his voice flat. "His name is Murray Crown. He is an ex-cop, fired from the force for doing his job a little too well. He was a very tough cookie, not so easily taken. But they took him."

19

"They?"

"It took more than one man to wreck your apartment, Peter. It has a gangland look to it—the killing, I mean. That—that missing tongue is a message to all the pigeons in town, the people who talk to honest cops and honest prosecutors. Did Crown talk to you, Peter? Did he provide you with material for your *Newsview* article?"

"I never saw him before, or heard of him."

"I'll tell you about him someday," Maxvil said. "I liked and admired him. This one is going to get special attention." He raised his eyes. "Maybe that empty mouth was meant as a message to you, friend."

There was no place to go, no place to sit down or lie down in the apartment. It was swarming with Maxvil's men from Homicide, dusting for fingerprints, searching for clear-enough footprints in the garden to make molds. Murray Crown's body had not been moved for a long time, waiting for the Medical Examiner to give the word.

Crown had been stabbed in the back, seven times to be exact, with a thin, very sharp blade. Without an autopsy the M.E. guessed that heart, lungs, and other vital organs had been penetrated. There must have been a moment of incredible violence, but it couldn't have taken Crown long to die. He had been too cruelly hurt.

There had been no particular effort by the killers to hide the way they had come and gone. There were at least four different sets of footprints leading to and from the rear of the garden to the board fence. Marks on the fence showed where they had climbed it. There was a separate set of prints coming in from the side of the garden that Maxvil had been able to identify as Crown's. There was no way to tell, yet, whether he had come first and been caught there by the killers, or whether he had followed them in and un-

20

derestimated his ability to cope with the situation.

Nathan Hale Jones appeared at the apartment shortly after midnight. He and his two bodyguards seemed strangely out of place with Maxvil's uniformed and plain-clothes crew. The two giant bodyguards wore baseball caps, bell-bottom trousers. One had on a bright orange shirt, the other was in Irish green. Nathan, Peter thought, looked like something out of a science fiction melodrama; black shoes, black trousers, black shirt, black glasses, and black face with its Fu Manchu decoration of mustache and beard. He and Maxvil seemed to know each other. Nathan gave the Lieutenant a theatrically elegant bow.

"Forgive me for invading your part of town, Lieutenant," he said.

"We need your help," Maxvil said.

"Not to identify the victim, if I can trust my intuition. It is Murray Crown, yes?"

"Yes."

"A man is a fool to play any kind of dangerous game alone in this day and age," Nathan said. He turned the black glasses on Peter. "I imagine you couldn't care less, Styles. Is it true about Grace?"

"It's not certain," Peter said, in that stranger's voice. "It's not certain but it appears to be true."

"So you may not be able to hear me," Nathan said. No word of regret, no sympathy. Perhaps this man understood that sympathy made it worse. "You may have guessed that Murray Crown is the man who bugged the telephone in the office of Anthony Larch, Insurance Broker."

"What's this?" Maxvil asked.

A naked light bulb was reflected in Nathan's black glasses. "There are too many balls in the air, Lieutenant. There is Grace, and there is a dead man in Peter's garden." He smiled, a bitter smile. "Have you found his tongue?

Maybe it could still talk."

"Would you mind very much dealing with facts?" Maxvil said. "What has Crown been up to? You say he bugged Tony Larch's phone?"

It was cold in those distant mountains, Peter thought. If she was alive, and hurt, and cold—

"You've seen Styles's story in today's *Newsview?*" Nathan asked Maxvil.

They're talking as though I'm not here, Peter thought. They know I can't concentrate on what concerns them. *All I want to be forever is your wife, your love—*

"You don't play the drug scene, Lieutenant," Nathan said. "You are departmentalized. You don't prevent crime, you only deal with it after it's been done. Crown was dropped from your white man's army because he tried to stop crime, not solve it like a puzzle."

"Lecture me some other time," Maxvil said. "While you moralize, the people who killed Crown are gaining time and distance on us."

"My apologies," Nathan said, dryly. "Crown was trying to save thousands of black people from the horrors of drug addiction. He knew and believed what we all know and believe in my world, that organized crime is behind the drug racket in Harlem. He believed, as we all believe, that the big dealers, the big pushers, are controlled by an organized family, the Larchesis. A favorite son, who calls himself Tony Larch, and who pretends to be in the insurance business, is the on-the-spot boss in Harlem. A white man, destroying his black customers."

"For the record," Maxvil said, "Larch does run a very successful and profitable insurance business."

"As a cover," Nathan said. "Crown was after him. Crown bugged his phone. On miles of tape he collected was a small fragment that alerted us to what is happening in the

22

Larkspur business. I came to Styles with the fragment; came because he is married to Grace, our friend. My friend and Murray Crown's friend."

Peter turned his head. "Grace knew Murray Crown?"

"Knew and trusted him."

"You didn't tell me that!"

"I couldn't mention Crown's name to you," Nathan said. "Not because I didn't trust you, Styles, but because it might have slipped out or been forced out of you. If it had, Crown was a dead man. The Larchesi family would have seen to that."

"Has seen to it," Maxvil said.

Grace's friend. "Why did he come here?" Peter asked.

"I wish I knew," Nathan said. His mouth was a thin slit in his black face. "I was out of touch early this evening. Crown called me two or three times, but I didn't get the message, so I didn't call him back. Your story was out on the streets, Styles, and I was observing the reactions. So I can only guess. I guess that Crown heard something on Larch's tapped phone that related to you, Styles. He wanted you warned. Since he couldn't reach me he decided to try to warn you himself. You were Grace's husband, you see. Like many people in my community he would have given his life for your Grace, Styles."

"It seems he did," Maxvil said.

"I never had any doubt," Nathan said, "that your story would hit the bull's-eye, Styles. I didn't think the reaction would be instant violence. If there was to be violence, I thought it would come much later on, when there was no other out for them."

"What 'them'?" Maxvil asked.

"The men who have stolen more than twenty million dollars from the Larkspur Fund," Nathan said.

"The Larchesi family?"

23

Nathan shook his head. "Tony Larch is just a weapon; a gun, a knife. He probably has a piece of the pie for his help, but the real conspirators are eating caviar and drinking champagne somewhere tonight—unless Styles's story has affected their appetites."

"Who are they?" Maxvil asked.

"I wish I could tell you," Nathan said. "What we know for sure is public knowledge. A banker named Walter Girard headed the fund drive. We know from Crown's tape that Girard set up Swiss bank accounts. And we know from that tape that someone involved has the first name of 'Tom.'"

"Newspapermen aren't ordinarily in danger for what they get into print," Maxvil said. "Take a potshot at a newspaperman and every reporter and news medium in the world is on your back. All the same," and his eyes shifted to Peter, "you'd better watch your step, man. These bastards who mutilated Crown were trying to tell you something."

"You go after Larch?" Peter asked. He found himself wavering along one road. Crown was Grace's friend. There was a linkage here. Since he couldn't go to her she would want him to help her friends.

Maxvil gestured toward the room, being carefully examined by his men. "If Larch was back of this you know how it will be, Peter. Larch was never here himself. He will have a perfect alibi. He will have been visiting an uncle in Jersey, and there will be fifteen witnesses to prove it. The men who were here a few hours ago are already underground, lost. If they represent a danger to Larch when we find them, they'll be dead. At best they're pawns in the game. Walter Girard and his fellow conspirators would appear to be the important pieces—did Crown suggest to you who they might be, Nathan?"

"Anyone from the mayor on down," Nathan said. "They could be bankers, brokers, industrialists, big shots in any business you care to name. For a share in twenty million bucks it could be almost anyone. Like it or not every man has his price. If I offered you a million dollars right here and now to let the Crown murder go unsolved, what would you say?"

"I'd tell you to go screw yourself," Maxvil said. "Less politely than that."

"That's nice to know," Nathan said. "There are at least three of us who won't sell out." He looked over his shoulder at his two giant bodyguards who hadn't moved or spoken. "There may be a little violence in Harlem, Lieutenant. If you check it out you'll find the victims are Larch's men—the pawns. I don't think we'll wait for you to get a grand jury indictment on those creeps. If you'll take advice, keep your eyes on Walter Girard. He's going to be running scared after Styles's piece. He may flush some other birds."

"You forget I'm a Homicide man," Maxvil said. "I'm tied to this killing here, even if it leads only to pawns."

Peter was astonished to hear himself say: "Leave Girard to me."

Peter had thought of himself as being able to face any kind of violence without being thrown out of control. As a journalist he had embarked on a crusade to hunt down the people in our society who violate the rules that make freedom and justice possible. You could always find ways and means to fight an enemy.

That night he had been thrown completely off the rails of his life. There was no way to fight the violence that had swallowed up Grace. You couldn't fight a mechanical

25

failure. You couldn't fight the intangible thing that was pilot error. You couldn't fight the whims of mountains winds, of unpredictable downdrafts. There was no way to fight back, no way to get even. There was no anesthesia for the pain.

Devery had said it was not final; that he must stay in one piece and keep working. It might be a day, a week, a month before he heard from Preston in the State Department that the wreckage had been found and that it was, at last, final. To bridge that time he must struggle to keep hope alive, like a pinpoint of light at the end of a long tunnel. She would have wanted him to help Nathan Jones and the dead Crown. So that was how he would manage until he knew that all hope was dead.

So, very slowly, he began to take stock of himself and the situation.

He knew he was close to physical exhaustion. There was no way to get any rest in the apartment. Maxvil's men would be there for hours. It was after one o'clock when Peter called the Players Club around the corner and found that there was a room available. He packed an overnight bag and walked to the club. Tommy, the night doorman, let him in, and he managed to avoid the bridge players who were still at their game in the bar. He took the old-fashioned elevator with a portrait of Sarah Bernhardt on its rear wall, to the top of the house.

He had taught himself over the years to sleep whenever the opportunity afforded. Tonight he couldn't make it work. He lay in bed, listening to the intermittent sounds of traffic around Gramercy Park. Some jerk in one of the Park apartments had a radio or a record player blaring out an endless rock beat. There seemed no way to shut out the visions of Crown's face, of Grace's loveliness, lost forever. They went round and round—until he must have dozed off because it was suddenly daylight. He glanced at his watch. It was after seven.

He got up, shaved, took a scalding-hot shower, and dressed. He was the only breakfaster in the grill room when he got there and took one of the round tables. The waiter gave him two morning papers with his coffee.

It was there again. The missing plane, the lost passengers, the lone woman being the wife of a famous journalist. He turned away from it and saw a story about Larkspur. The Mayor was demanding a thorough investigation as a result of the story in *Newsview*. There was a picture of Walter Girard, a distinguished man in his early fifties, grey at the temples, a charming smile on his face. The picture had been taken some time ago. Next to it was the picture of an exciting-looking blond girl, Elaine Summers, Girard's young wife, who was starring in *Glamor Town* on Broadway. Neither she nor Girard had been available for comment when the paper had gone to press. A few contributors to the fund had been reached and expressed alarm. One of them was Theodore Osborne McCauley, a city councilman, who admitted he had given ten thousand dollars to the fund. "The District Attorney must start an immediate investigation," the Councilman said. "But I would stake my life on Walter Girard's complete honesty!" A hell of a lot of people had staked a hell of a lot on Girard's honesty.

The waiter brought bacon and eggs. Peter was only halfway through when the waiter returned with word that Peter was wanted on the telephone. He took the call on the phone behind the deserted bar.

It was Maxvil. "Get some rest?" he asked.

"A little."

"We're just about through here, Peter. I called because the District Attorney's office has been trying to reach you."

"I gather from the morning paper that he's in the act."

"The morning paper doesn't have it all, Peter." Maxvi
sounded odd. "You must have been really on target, boy
Walter Girard committed suicide in his office some tim
during the night. Cleaning woman found him about an hou
ago. He put a handgun in his mouth and pulled the trigger."

CHAPTER 3

YESTERDAY HAD BEEN a Wednesday. It was matinee day for the hit musical, *Glamor Town*. Elaine Summers, Walter Girard's bride of eighteen months, had a special routine on matinee days. She didn't leave the theater after the matinee performance. She had a light supper brought to the theater. Sometimes she ate it alone, sometimes Girard joined her. She needed to recharge herself after singing and dancing some fourteen numbers in the show. The management hired a special security boy on those Wednesday afternoons. For fifteen minutes after the matinee's final curtain Elaine held court for friends who had been in the audience. Then she excused herself, and her dressing room door was guarded. Nobody was allowed in except her husband for a two-hour stretch. There was also the boy from Sardi's who brought her supper.

Elaine Summers had knocked Broadway on its collective ears in *Glamor Town*. Old-timers called her a present-day Carole Lombard, who could also sing and dance. There had been pages of interviews with her in magazines and the Sunday press. She was a girl with wit and warmth, rumored to be remarkably amusing in the use of four-letter words which she handled without a blush, or a trace of self-consciousness. She was half Walter Girard's age. He must be, people thought, the luckiest man in town to have won this extraordinary girl for himself. Interviewers always asked her how she happened to have married a man old enough to be her father.

"The first one to hand me any Freudian crap gets it right between the eyes," she told the drama man from the *Times*. "I married Walter because I love him. I know that when I'm fifty he'll be seventy-nine. So what? I care about today. I could be run over by a taxi tomorrow. When I'm fifty I'll worry about myself and not how old Walter is."

Peter's story on the possible swindle in Larkspur appeared on the newsstands and in the subscribers' mail on Thursday morning. The resulting outcry didn't begin to gather momentum until late in the day. Walter Girard, looking strained and tired, had turned up at the theater to have supper with his wife. He must have told her then what was in the wind, if she hadn't already heard it from someone. He had gone from the theater, shortly before seven in the evening, to his office on Wall Street. The building was deserted then except for the night maintenance crew, which included a guard who was stationed by the bank of elevators. People sometimes came back to the building to work at night, and they were required to sign in. Girard had signed in at ten minutes past seven. The guard was required to write down the time someone came, and later the time they left. Girard had signed in, but he had never signed out. The guard had paid no attention to this. The plush offices of Walter Girard & Associates, Investment Bankers, had a small bedroom, bath, and kitchenette complex in it. It wasn't unusual for one of the executives to work at night and to, eventually, sleep there. In the days before his marriage to Elaine Summers, Girard had often stayed overnight.

The cleanup crew arrived at about 5 A.M. Jim Whelan, the guard, told them that Girard was sleeping in the office apartment. The mop-and-pail brigade went upstairs, knowing that they would skip the soundproofed sleeping quarters because Mr. Girard was there. But Mr. Girard was not in the special apartment. He was sprawled across his desk in his private office, his brains spattered over the blotter pad. A .38 police special was still clutched in his right hand. It was his gun and he had a license to carry it. The only other thing out of the ordinary in the room was that a big metal wastebasket had been brought in from one of the outer offices. It was half-filled with the ashes from burned papers.

"It looks open and shut, Peter," the District Attorney said. This little grey man, Jerome Marshall, long-time holder of the office, so mild outwardly, so tough at his job, was an old personal friend of Peter's. There had been a brief moment when Peter arrived at the D.A.'s office in answer to a request from Marshall when the friend had to say something about a missing plane, a missing love. Knowing Peter, Jerry Marshall had spoken softly, very briefly, and gone directly to the point. "We've talked to Mrs. Girard—Elaine Summers. It's very rough for her."

"I can guess," Peter said, his eyes turned away.

"He went to the theater between the matinee and evening performance to see her," Marshall said. "He had a copy of the magazine with your story in it. She hadn't seen it and no one had mentioned it to her. If people in the company knew about it they kept it from her."

"The show must go on," Peter said.

"Maybe something like that. But Girard made her read it, she says. He told her, she says, that he was innocent of any wrong-doing. But he said there were some coincidences in your story—that's his word, 'coincidences'—that distressed him. He told her he was going to his office to meet with associates of his. He might not be home that night. She must trust him, believe in him. If there was something wrong, as your story suggested, he would see it through right to the end of the line. Again those are his words; 'see it through right to the end of the line.'"

"She believes he was innocent?"

"Convinced. She will prove his innocence if it takes her the rest of her life."

"The suicide seems like a certain confession," Peter said.

"She says it wasn't a suicide. She says somebody killed him and made it look like suicide."

"Who came to see him? What 'associates'?"

"Nobody came to see him. Nobody but Girard went up to that office last night. Nobody unaccounted for came to or left the building."

"So Elaine Summers loves her husband and has to insist on his innocence for her own sanity," Peter said.

Marshall leaned back in his desk chair, fumbling with a pipe which he never got around to lighting. "Maxvil's told me what happened at your place. Was Murray Crown the source of your information on Larkspur?"

"He was, but I didn't know it until after I found him dead last night. Someone had bugged Tony Larch's telephone in Harlem, trying to nail him on a drug charge. A lot of conversations were taped, and in the middle of them was a conversation between two unidentified men, one of them named Tom, which suggested the money from Larkspur had been transferred to Swiss bank accounts. That was my starting point. Once you started looking there were a great many suspicious details that seemed to tie in. Good enough to write a piece asking questions. My source at the beginning was Nathan Hale Jones. We met him once before, Jerry, during that hot summer killing."

"Extraordinary man."

"He told me tonight, after I found Crown, that he was the man who had supplied the tape."

"Why did Crown come to your place?"

"No idea."

"Did whoever searched your apartment find that tape?"

"Mine is only a tape of a tape. Crown, I suppose, had the original. My copy is in the safe at *Newsview*. My notes are there too. There was nothing in my apartment to find."

"Except Crown," Marshall said. He moved restlessly in his chair, fiddling with his pipe. "You're handling a very hot potato, Peter."

"I guess. But Girard's suicide should give you what you need to dig a lot deeper than I can."

"You a movie fan?" Marshall asked, unexpectedly.

"Of sorts."

"I've seen Elaine Summers in half a dozen films. She's pretty amazing."

"So her husband was a thief. That doesn't make her any less amazing."

Marshall smiled, a wry little smile. "Someone like that you've seen so often in films, you get the strange feeling that you know them when you come face to face. I listened to her this morning and I kept feeling she was a friend. I—I wanted to help her. Sound cockeyed?"

"Maybe not."

"Girard killed himself—and yet she's so damned certain he didn't. She blames you."

"Me?"

"She says you arranged to get him killed—with your article. I think it would be a kindness if she was made to face the truth. If you told her what your article was based on, she might have to do just that. Otherwise she'll go on trying to prove the impossible. Nothing good can come of that, and she just might stumble onto something that would be dangerous to Girard's fellow conspirators. Then she'd be in big trouble."

"You want me to talk to her?"

"She wants to talk to you. I said I'd ask. Every reporter in town is trying to get to her. No dice. She wants you."

"Maybe you should provide me with a bulletproof vest."

"You may need another kind of armor," Marshall said. "This may be one of the most alluring woman you've ever met."

Peter smiled at his friend. "You're a big phony, you know that."

Marshall looked childishly innocent. "I don't get you."

"You're really not intertested in doing Elaine Summers a kindness. You need her help in digging into this Larkspur conspiracy, and as long as she's convinced her husband is innocent, that somebody killed him and he wasn't a suicide, she isn't going to be any use to you. She won't see anything suspicious in anything he ever did or said. He was innocent and so his friends were innocent—his doctors, his lawyers, his merchants, his chiefs. You want me to break her down so she'll get useful to you."

"It would still be a kindness to her in the long run to stop her from chasing a fantasy," Marshall said.

Peter stood up. "I'll talk to her because I want her help, too. My story has to take a new slant now. Stealing money is one thing. It's one of today's favorite indoor sports. Killing a man and cutting out his tongue to cover that theft is something else again."

"Maxvil thinks it was a gangland job," Marshall said.

"Maxvil also said that Tony Larch was just a weapon, a gun, a knife, paid for by someone else. The conspirators paid the price, approved the job. They're the ones I want."

34

His voice shook. "Crown was Grace's friend. Squaring his account may be the last thing I can do for her."

Marshall put his pipe down down on the desk. "You want a permit to carry a gun?"

"Why?"

"You may need one. Crown is dead. They can only be hung once. Your typewriter is more dangerous to them than Maxvil's homicide boys. With twenty million bucks at stake you don't have any kind of journalistic immunity, Peter."

Peter looked away. "I've got to be doing something, Jerry; something tough and difficult. Otherwise I'll go quietly out of my mind."

Marshall knew better than to go into a sympathy routine.

No doubt about it, she was something very special. Some of it could be acting a part. After all, she was a brilliant actress. Physically she was sustained by some kind of high-voltage internal electricity. She was tallish, slim, beautifully built. Peter thought he had never seen such intense blue eyes. She was, he thought, not only able to read the maker's name on the inside of his shirt collar, she was seeing right into the center of him to what made him tick. No wonder she could take a theater audience and twist them around her little finger. She had a magic.

"I don't thank you for coming here, Styles," she said. Her voice was controlled, energized. "You want to talk to me as much as I want to talk to you."

Walter Girard had owned his own house on upper Fifth Avenue. It was furnished with a kind of taste that Peter admired. There were fine paintings. In the library where they talked there was a brilliant Wyeth and a glowing portrait of Elaine by Gordon Stevenson. The furniture was early American. But there was no quality of a museum or an art gallery. Girard had bought things he liked and

35

he had lived with them. They hadn't been a means of showing his friends how rich he was or how cultured. It told
Peter something about the man he hadn't expected.

Elaine had indicated a chair for Peter, but she herself
paced restlessly around the book-lined room. She was wearing a dark blue knit dress that set off her magnificent figure.
Her hair was golden, not blonde, worn loose and shoulder-
length. She moved, Peter thought, like a sleek black pan-
ther, prowling and prowling.

There was a third person in the room, a heavy-set jowly
man wearing a tweed jacket and smoking cigarettes in a
chain. He had been introduced as Andrew Callahan, Girard's lawyer and personal friend. It was a snubbed-nosed
Irish face, and the deep lines at the corners of his eyes and
mouth suggested habitual good humor. This morning he
was a man feeling pain. He was also, Peter guessed, a man
who was dealing with a massive hangover.

"You and I have something in common, Styles," Elaine
said, moving in a circle around Peter's chair as if she needed
to study him from all angles. "We have both suffered the
same kind of loss within hours of each other. I don't believe
in mourning, and apparently you don't either. Mourning is
for self-pitiers, people who feel sorry for themselves and
not the dead one. Andrew doesn't agree. Andrew thinks we
should hold an Irish wake for Walter. I don't want to
mourn him. I want to find the sonofabitch who killed him!"

The language was a mild jolt.

"Elaine!" Callahan said. His voice was husky from liquor
and tobacco.

"I listened to all the crap the District Attorney dished
out," Elaine said. "I knew Walter. I loved him. I slept in
his bed with him. When you make love to a man you know
how honest he is and how much of a faker he is. Walter
was dead honest. He wasn't a quitter. If he had trouble to

36

face, he'd face it. He wouldn't run out like a cowardly jerk. You made the trouble, Styles, that got him killed. They tell me you're not a sensation-seeking, yellow journalist. So tell me what you know that you didn't put in your article." She had wound up facing him, her eyes blazing.

"Elaine, you're not being fair to Mr. Styles," Callahan said. "I'm afraid he did the job that any good journalist would do. He heard rumors. He followed them up." He looked at Peter. "We started checking yesterday afternoon when your story first appeared, Mr. Styles. There seems to be no question that a huge sum of money is missing from the Larkspur Fund. I talked to Walter late in the afternoon. He sounded distracted, like a man who didn't know which way to turn. He refused to see me, to talk to me."

"He was distracted because he suddenly knew that some friends of his had done him in," Elaine said. "Maybe he thought you were one of them, Andrew."

"My dear girl, surely you don't think—"

"I think I am going to find out the truth," Elaine said. "Well, Styles?"

"Your husband isn't the only man who died violently last night," Peter said. He felt his jaw muscles tighten. "The man who put me on the trail of this story was murdered in the garden of my apartment. Somebody took the time, after they'd killed him, to cut out his tongue."

"Christ Almighty!" Callahan said. He looked around as if he was searching for a drink.

Elaine stood tall and straight in front of Peter. "So two men who guessed at the truth were silenced," she said. "So why don't you get off your butt, Styles, and go after the real story?"

"Oh, I promise you I'll go right to the end of the line

with it."

"That's what Walter said and they killed him," Elaine said.

"My dear, dear Elaine, you simply can't bypass the facts," Callahan said. "Walter went to his office around seven o'clock. He signed in with the guard. Nobody came to see him. He apparently burned a quantity of papers in that metal basket. He took his own gun out of the desk drawer where he kept it and shot himself with it."

"Never!" Elaine said.

"But he was alone. Nobody else went up to the offices!"

"That's what the guard says."

"That's what the record says—the sign-in sheet."

"Listen to me, Andrew!" Elaine's voice had a knife edge to it. "If there are millions of dollars at stake here, the guard could have been bought. Every man has his price at some level. Or the guard just could be honest. But he's human. At some point he had to go to the john and somebody slipped past his post."

"Not impossible," Peter said. Her intensity carried conviction.

"So, Andrew, you knew that Walter kept a gun in the office. Don't flinch! A lot of people knew he kept a gun in his office. One of the miserable bastards who betrayed him—Styles's tongue-cutter-outer—took Walter's gun when he was off guard and killed him with it. There's no other way it could have been."

Callahan drew a deep breath. "Your loyalty to Walter is a wonderful thing, Elaine. But the facts, my dear. It's a dreadful shock to all of us, but there it is."

Elaine faced Peter. "While Andrew tries to prove his friend's guilt, will you help me to prove the truth, Styles?"

"The truth is my business," Peter said.

"Stop fidgeting, Andrew!" Elaine said impatiently. "If

you want a drink, help yourself. I don't give a damn that it's only ten o'clock in the morning. It's your liver." She turned back to Peter. "You can't approach this with my certainty, Styles. I knew my man. You didn't. So I start one step ahead of you. I *know* he didn't kill himself."

"According to Jerry Marshall your husband came to the theater to see you in the break between the matinee and the evening performance," Peter said.

"He did, and oh my God, he was shattered, Styles. You did that to him. He had your goddamned article with him and he showed it to me. I might have killed you, you bastard, if I could have gotten to you at that moment. I saw a man with his whole lifetime crumbling around him."

"Motive for suicide," Callahan said. He had taken Elaine at her word and was filling a glass at the liquor cabinet in the corner. "You have to see that, Elaine."

"A motive for an honest man to find out who had given him the business," she said.

"Marshall says he told you he was going to his office to meet some of his associates," Peter said. "What associates?"

"He didn't use the word 'associates,'" Elaine said. "What he actually said was 'I'm going to have it out with some of the pricks who must have done this to me.' I asked him who they were. He said, 'People we've thought of as friends. But which one or ones is the question. Believe in me, darling.' That's the last thing he said to me. 'Believe in me, darling.' Well, I damn well do!"

"And you don't know who these alleged friends were?"

"Walter had hundreds of friends."

"But connected with the Larkspur Fund," Peter said.

Elaine turned to Callahan, who was still at the liquor cabinet. "Andrew has that answer."

Callahan tilted his head back to swallow a shot. He put the empty glass down hard on the cabinet, like a man who had made a decision.

"I was Walter's lawyer," he said, "and the lawyer for his firm. I had no professional connection with the Larkspur Fund, but of course Walter talked about it a lot. He headed the drive for money; he got some of the larger donations personally. But there were dozens of people who headed up committees to work in different sections of the city."

"I'm not very much concerned with who raised the money," Peter said. "Who handled it after it was collected?"

Callahan looked unhappy. "Walter's bank was the depository," he said. "There was an executive committee set up to handle the details. Walter was its chairman. There was a staff made up of accountants, building experts, a project director, a treasurer. There was a board of directors. Walter was on that board. Its chairman was Theodore McCauley."

"McCauley's on the City Council, isn't he? I thought the city had nothing to do with Larkspur."

"It doesn't. Ted McCauley, like a lot of other people, considered Larkspur a community venture worth supporting. Dollar-a-year men."

"Can you get me a list of all these committeemen, the experts, the accountants?"

"No sweat," Callahan said. "In view of what's happened these names will all be very public, God help them. Early this morning, when Walter was found, there was a quick look into the records at the bank by McCauley and the accountants and the lawyers for the fund. I was called in because I represented Walter and the bank. The money, large gobs of it, is gone, Mr. Styles, just as you suspected."

"How could it have been withdrawn—transferred to Swiss accounts?"

"If that's what happened," Callahan said. "I mean, they

40

don't know yet about the Swiss accounts or if they exist. But Walter could have arranged a transfer of money. There would have been records of it. I'm afraid those records are what he burned in the wastebasket."

"That is unadulterated crap, and you know it, Andrew!" Elaine said.

A telephone rang somewhere in the distance.

"Who else could have arranged a transfer?" Peter asked.

"I'm afraid no one could have arranged it without Walter's knowing it," Callahan said.

A maid appeared in the doorway. "A telephone call for you, Mrs. Girard."

"I told you I wasn't taking calls, Marcia. Every reporter in the country is trying to get to me," Elaine said.

"It's Mr. Carrington," the maid said. "He needs to know whether you want tonight's performance of the play canceled."

"Poor Miles. He must be sweating blood. I'll talk to him." She started for the door.

"You will cancel, of course," Callahan said.

"We damn well won't cancel," Elaine said. "But tonight I make a curtain speech about Walter!" And she disappeared.

Callahan turned back to the drink cabinet. "It's a terrible thing to lose a friend you loved and trusted," he said. "But to discover that he was a villain of sorts! Jesus!" He poured himself a stiff jolt and drank half of it. "This must be pretty awful for you, Mr. Styles. Is the news about your wife definite?"

"They haven't found the plane," Peter said in a flat voice. "Until they do there may be some faint hope."

"I should think you'd want to be over there," Callahan said.

"I tried. State Department regulations. Until they know

41

for certain, one way or the other—"

"Nothing one can say."

"Don't try. I'm grateful to have something to work at."

Callahan tossed off the second half of his drink. "Elaine is a wonderful girl," he said. "Don't be turned off by her tough language."

"I'm not."

"None of Walter's friends thought it would work. Older man marries young girl. He was twenty-nine years older. Old man tries to satisfy young sex queen. She is a kind of sex symbol to the public, you know. We figured she'd tire of him pretty fast, or he'd die of a heart attack. Of course she didn't marry him for money. She's made a fortune in films, handled it well. I know because I take care of her affairs. She really loved Walter."

"Was he broke? Did he need money badly enough to steal it?"

"Walter is worth several million dollars in his own right. He was a very shrewd money man. He made good investments for himself and for his clients. He gave a hundred grand to Larkspur."

"So why would he steal, or help to steal, a fortune he didn't need? Can you make that make sense, Callahan?"

"I would have said it was unthinkable," Callahan said. "But I suppose we'll find out when we start digging deep into his personal affairs."

"So you're convinced there is something wrong, hidden away from us, and that he did kill himself?"

Callahan shrugged. He sounded very tired. "What else?" he said.

Elaine came back from the phone. "Well, Styles?" She stood in the doorway, feet spread apart, her arms crossed.

"It's my job to go all the way with this story, Mrs. Girard."

"It's just possible, when you come up with the truth, Styles, I may sue you and your magazine for everything you've got, including the fillings in your teeth!"

"If I had never written my story, Mrs. Girard, sooner or later the conspiracy to hijack the Larkspur money would have been revealed. I may have made it happen a little sooner, that's all."

"But you accused Walter."

Peter felt a curious sympathy for this fighting woman. "I'm going to tell you something," he said, "that won't be a secret any longer now that the case has broken. In Harlem there is a man named Tony Larch. He is the son of one of the top Syndicate figures in this city."

"Syndicate?"

"Organized crime, Mrs. Girard. His front is an insurance business, but actually he is suspected of handling a huge business in narcotics."

"What has that to do with Walter?"

"I don't know. But he is indirectly responsible for my getting onto this story."

"That's the Larchesi family, isn't it?" Callahan asked. He was at the bottle again. "Vittorio Larchesi?"

"The son Americanized his name," Peter said. "Tony Larch. People in the black community have been trying to expose Larch, Mrs. Girard. A former policeman tapped his phone. He had records of hundreds of calls, most of them legitimate insurance business. One of them that seemed disconnected with the drug business or the insurance business was between two men, unidentified. I can tell you exactly how it went because I've played it fifty times, trying to identify the voices. The first voice says: 'Tom? I thought you should know that Girard has arranged for two numbered Swiss bank accounts.' Second voice: 'Great.' First voice: 'The money will have been transferred in a few

43

days. It will certainly be a few months before anybody smells a rat.' Second voice: 'And then?' First voice: 'Then we proceed as planned.' "

Elaine stared at him, her lips parted. "That tape actually exists?"

"It was brought to me by someone in the black community who was concerned about Larkspur. I followed up. The contractor has a dummy setup at the site. There were some other oddities that made me believe the tape was for real. I know it now."

"Because of what happened to Walter?"

"I knew it before that, Mrs. Girard. You see, the man who was murdered and mutilated in my garden last night was the man who bugged Tony Larch's phone. The men who killed him were searching my apartment for that tape, or any other notes or documents I might have. Fortunately there was nothing there for them to find. But Crown, the ex-cop, either walked in on them or was brought there by them and left for me to find. Left as a warning to me."

"My God!" Elaine said.

"Does the name Tom mean anything to either of you?" Peter asked. "A friend of Girard's, a business associate?"

Elaine shook her head slowly.

"I know half a dozen Toms," Callahan said. "None of them could possibly be your voice."

"The purpose of my article was to get somebody frightened into showing his hand," Peter said. "I didn't anticipate this kind of violence. I wanted the right people to ask questions. I wanted someone to have to check the Larkspur Fund to see if it was intact. I mentioned your husband's name, partly because it was the only one I had, partly because, if he was honest, he would immediately investigate. If he was a part of the conspiracy and had set up Swiss bank accounts in which to hide the money, he

44

would move to cover his tracks. Either way he'd have to reveal himself. If he killed himself, he's admitted his guilt. If, as you think, Mrs. Girard, he was murdered, we're going to have to prove it to clear him."

"What about you?" Elaine asked. "Aren't you in danger?"

"I suppose, if I keep digging, I am," Peter said. "But there are going to be so many people digging now it won't help them much to polish me off."

"So help Walter! Help restore the faith his friends had in him!"

"I'll keep after the truth, Mrs. Girard." Peter started for the door.

"Styles!" Elaine stopped him. The corners of her mouth moved in a bitter-sweet smile. "There is a young man who might be helpful to you. His name is Gary Lehman. He handled the public relations job for the Larkspur Fund. He knows everyone involved with the project, and where most of the bodies are buried. You agree, Andrew?"

"An insufferable wise guy," Callahan said. "But he does know people."

"He's been trying to get me into the circular bed he has in his apartment since the day I married Walter," Elaine said. "I may say I come under the head of unfinished business with him. Tell him I sent you. He may think I'm making a pass at him."

"And are you?" Peter asked.

She looked him up and down, coolly. "There are more interesting fish in the sea," she said.

It was after eleven in the morning when Peter walked out of the Girard house and onto Fifth Avenue. It was a hot, hazy day, no different on the surface than any other summer day in the city. Children played in the park. Chic-

45

looking women walked downtown toward the shopping area. The traffic seemed lazy and unhurried in this part of town. He and Grace used to come up here in the summers to see the Shakespeare-in-the-Park productions. Good days, good times; and now his whole world darkened by violence.

He would have to get his cleaning woman, Mrs. Markell, to help him put the apartment together again if Maxvil was through with it. The tailor would have to repair his clothes. He'd have to find an upholsterer to deal with the slashed furniture.

And he had to find and face a killer. The whole city knew by now that he was involved. He had a strange feeling that he might be watched. He turned to look behind him. A pretty girl in a filmy summer dress smiled at him. The city seemed as it always was and always would be.

Maxvil was still in the apartment when Peter got there, but not alone. It was Mrs. Markell's morning, and she was bullying the detective and the two men who were left there with him.

"You'd think with the taxes we pay they wouldn't let a thing like this happen," she said to Peter. "I've found a couple of clean sheets that weren't slashed to pieces and made up your bed, Mr. Styles. And oh my God, the news about Mrs. Styles!"

"We have to keep hoping, Bessie."

"Praying, that's what I'm doing, Mr. Styles."

He saw that she'd gotten most of the books back in the cases, the drawers back in his desk.

"Things probably aren't just the way they were, Mr. Styles, but I've done my best."

"Thanks, Bessie. I'm very grateful."

"There's coffee in the kitchen. I'll get you some."

"Quite an old girl," Maxvil said, as Bessie disappeared. He looked done in. He was standing by the French windows

46

frowning out at the garden. The remains of Murray Crown were long gone.

"You turn up anything?" Peter asked.

"Fingerprints that we haven't matched with anything yet," Maxvil said. "Molds of footprints that don't yet match anyone's feet. The certainty that Crown was killed here. When we moved him we found your flower bed soaked with blood. You still don't know why he came here, Peter?"

"No idea."

Maxvil fished a cigarette out of his pocket and lit it. "Let me tell you about this man Crown," he said. "He was an old-school cop. He was big, tough, and very determined. The courts have made it rugged for the old-school boys. Lawyers spend weeks preparing a case, and the courts spend weeks weighing the evidence, but a cop, standing outside a door behind which a killer is hiding, has to make his decision on the spot. The old-school cop smashed his way in, and he didn't stop to think how hard he'd hit his man, or worry about reciting the criminal's rights and privileges before he slugged him. The new cop, because he isn't sure there's anyone behind him, backing him up, stands outside the door reciting the penal code to the man he's after. Crown belonged to another time; he went after his man without worrying whether someone would call him brutal. He moved hard and he moved tough because experience told him if he didn't he might get killed. New-school cops are getting killed every day on our streets. The old-timers were harder to take."

"And yet they took him," Peter said.

"That's the puzzle," Maxvil said. "Crown was tough, but he wasn't careless. Yet he seems to have walked right into this."

"Why was he fired from the force?"

47

"He charged into a Harlem apartment where two white men were holed up. Two white men and a million dollars worth of heroin. Crown didn't stop to tell them their rights. He half-killed them both. They were spreading misery among his people—the black people. They were Larchesi people, the two men Crown took, and the Syndicate has political muscle. Crown was set down for brutalizing his suspects, not informing them of their rights before he took them."

"You agree with Nathan Jones that it was probably Larchesi's people who were here last night?" Peter asked.

"I think it's likely. The mutilation of Crown makes me think so. I don't think it's going to be easy to prove it. There are maybe a couple of dozen people in Harlem who would talk to me under other circumstances. A dead Crown with his tongue cut out has turned them to stone. Someone may talk to Nathan, but will he talk to me?" Maxvil took a deep drag on his cigarette. "Looks like your story set off an explosion. Girard's suicide just about nails it down."

"His wife thinks he was murdered," Peter said.

Maxvil's tired eyes widened. Peter told him about his visit to Elaine. "She's half-sold me," Peter said. "You know somebody named Gary Lehman?"

"Public relations man? Sure, I know him. A very shrewd guy. A very smart guy. Great lady's man. He might even be able to sell you the Brooklyn Bridge, that's how good a salesman he is. He promoted the Larkspur Fund, didn't he?"

Peter nodded. "He might be able to tell me something Elaine thinks."

"He might be in on the swindle himself," Maxvil said. "Lehman comes first with Lehman. He'll do what he thinks will pay off for him in the end, no more, no less. If he's in on the swindle, he'll take you to nowhere by way of Alaska."

Peter's mouth tightened. "It can't hurt to listen. I don't have to go where he leads."

"You'll have to be as smart as he is not to," Maxvil said.

Gary Lehman operated out of an office on Madison Avenue, not far from *Newsview*'s. Peter, reaching a switchboard operator, was put through to young Mr. Lehman the moment he gave his name.

"Nice to talk to you, Peter Styles," Lehman said. "I half-expected you might call one of these days."

"Oh?"

"Anybody interested in Larkspur would be bound to talk to me sooner or later," Lehman said. He sounded young and full of bounce. "Maybe I should be sitting at your feet. I spend a year and a half building something up, and you knock it down with one three-thousand-word piece in *Newsview*."

"I haven't finished," Peter said. "I might not have called you on my own initiative. I suspect everybody on the inside of Larkspur."

"Look, dad, don't throw at the batter's head," Lehman said chuckling.

"I was advised to call you by Elaine Summers."

"You're kidding! I should call her, I know, but I just didn't have the heart. How is she taking it?"

"Well. She doesn't believe the suicide story. She thinks Girard was murdered."

Lehman whistled. "So that's how she takes it! She comes out fighting. What a doll!"

"She mentioned your circular bed."

"Oh ho! I think we should have a face-to-face, Peter. I'm supposed to play a squash match at the Athletic Club in about twenty-five minutes. I should have polished off my boy by one o'clock. I'll buy you lunch there."

49

"Why not."

"Peter?"

"Yes."

"In just what connection did Elaine mention my circular bed?"

"She said you'd been trying to get her into it since the day she was married."

"You can't blame a guy for trying. I have the feeling that one might be the highlight of a lifetime. Do you think, friend, she was trying to send me a message of some kind?"

"I think she was asking for help," Peter said.

"See you at one o'clock at the New York A.C.," Lehman said.

Maxvil had gone, and Bessie Markell was trying to put the kitchen in shape. Peter went into the bedroom to see if he could find some fresh clothes that had been left in one piece by last night's searchers. He found some slacks and a blue linen jacket.

The phone rang and he answered it at the bedside table.

"Mr. Peter Styles?" An operator's voice. "Washington, D.C., calling."

Peter's heart thudded against his ribs. Here it was. The final news. His mouth was dry.

"Mr. Styles?" Another operator. "Mr. Preston at the State Department."

"Peter?"

Peter moistened his lips. "They found her?" he asked.

"No, Peter. No! There's no news from out there. That's to say, the news is that they haven't found any trace of the plane so far. But the weather's very bad. Visibility almost zero."

"Why did you call?" Peter asked, breathing again.

"You seem to have friends in high places," Preston said.

"Meaning?"

50

"I can arrange for you to go out to Saigon. Someone put the heat on my superiors. They don't love you for the pressure, but you've got your way. When can you take off?"

"Just a minute," Peter said. "I haven't applied any pressure. I haven't talked to anyone about wanting to go except you. Was it Frank Devery?"

"You mean you don't know?"

"No idea."

"Big-shot New York lawyer," Preston said. "We owe him some favors. He's handled some sticky situations for us at the United Nations. Andrew Callahan. You know him, of course."

Peter felt the small hairs rising on the back of his neck. "I met him less than two hours ago," he said. "He was able to arrange this for me?"

"Seems like."

"I'll call him and thank him," Peter said. He drew a deep breath. "But I don't think I'll go, Charlie. You were right yesterday. There isn't anything I can do out there. Of course if they find Grace—"

"They'll get her here as fast as you could get out there," Preston said.

"Thanks anyway."

"Don't thank me. Thank your friend Callahan."

Peter put down the telephone. So Callahan wanted him out of town, away from the Larkspur conspiracy! He was expected to be so eager to go that he wouldn't give Callahan's motive a second thought. Just a nice guy doing a nice favor? Was that possible? Every instinct Peter had refused to buy it.

He reached for the phone book and looked up Callahan's office number. When he reached it he was told that Mr. Callahan would not be in the office today.

"This is Peter Styles. Do you think I might still find him at Mrs. Girard's?"

"Just a minute, Mr. Styles."

And, by some miracle, here was Callahan. "Hello, Styles. I hope your call means they were able to fix the trip for you."

"They were," Peter said. "It was a terribly nice thing for you to do."

"Not at all. I knew how you must be feeling. Every now and then it comes time for someone to pay a debt. The State Department owes me."

"While I appreciate it deeply," Peter said, "I thought I should tell you that I'm not going."

"Oh?" Callahan's voice went suddenly flat.

"They've made it pretty clear to me that I wouldn't be able to help in the search for Grace. The best way to retain my sanity is to do my job here."

"Well, it's your decision, old man. I just thought—"

"And I'm grateful," Peter said.

He put down the phone and stood staring at it. Why would Callahan be so eager to get him away from New York? It was too late to do anything to cover up the conspiracy. Peter's presence or absence would not prevent the District Attorney's office from digging to the very bottom. Peter had lit a fuse, but now the explosion had taken place and he was only one of hundreds of reporters who would be after the story. Why this elaborate maneuver to get him away?

He glanced at his watch. It was time to head uptown to meet Gary Lehman.

CHAPTER 4

GARY LEHMAN WAS someone you were expected to like on sight, and it wasn't just a calculated act he put on. He was young, full of bubbling physical energy. He was as tall as Peter, but ash blond. He was tanned from much outdoors. His hair, bleached from the sun, was worn longish, but beautifully styled. The pink linen suit he was wearing when Peter met him in the club's grill room was a mod-tailor's creative gem. His smile was wide, very white, and completely disarming.

"Great pleasure to meet you, Peter. I've been a fan of yours for years," he said. His handshake was firm but not bone-crushing. He must, Peter thought, have little difficulty in luring ladies into that circular bed. His bright face clouded. "I didn't know, when I talked to you on the phone, about your wife. I hope the news isn't all bad. There is some hope?"

"As long as they haven't been found," Peter said. "You win your match?"

"Yeah, but it was a little tougher than I expected. I'm panting for a double, very dry, martini. So much for health and exercise. How about you?"

"I'll risk a single."

Lehman led the way to a corner table in the crowded grill room and ordered the drinks, writing the order on a slip the waiter brought him. "We don't have to eat til we're ready," Lehman said, "but we might as well order. I recommend the cold poached salmon with Béarnaise sauce."

"Sounds good."

"Toasted Italian bread, salad, and a chilled white wine?"

"If you can talk while you're eating," Peter said. He was studying Lehman, trying to guess which side of the fence he might be on.

Lehman handed the slip to the waiter. "Hold the food, George, until we've had at least a second drink." A bar boy brought the cocktails and Lehman raised his glass. "To your wife's safe return," he said. He sipped his drink. "You really blew this town wide open yesterday with your story, Peter. I wish to God I knew how you got on the track of it. It's been right under my nose for months and I never dreamed there was anything fishy going on."

"You haven't seen the afternoon paper or heard the radio?" Peter asked.

"Something more?"

"An ex-policeman named Murray Crown was murdered in the garden of my apartment last night," Peter said. "He was my source. Somebody cut out his tongue."

"Sweet Judas!" Lehman said.

The bugged telephone was no longer a secret and Peter told Lehman about the tape. "My first question to you, Mr. Lehman, is who could 'Tom' be?"

"This is an age of first names, Peter," Lehman said. "Please make it Gary." He took a deeper swallow of his martini. "Your friend Crown, and then Walter's suicide! A night to remember. God! But you asked me about a
54

'Tom.'" He frowned. "It doesn't ring a bell. The key people in the Larkspur setup are Girard—was Girard; City Councilman Ted McCauley; our dapper Deputy Mayor, Vincent Boswell; Lucius Blocker, the executive director of the project; and Edgar Bracket, the treasurer. There's a long list of directors, but most all of them are just prestige names, men who don't really know what's cooking."

"No Tom on that list," Peter said. "What about Andrew Callahan?"

"You've met our Andrew?"

"This morning at Mrs. Girard's."

"Comforting the widow, eh?" Gary laughed. "Like me, he's been trying to comfort Elaine for months—if you'll accept that word. But, seriously, Andrew was very close to Walter; his personal lawyer, the bank's lawyer. One of the smartest legal minds in town. He totters now and then from a little too much sour mash, but if you're ever in big trouble with the law there'd be no one better than Andrew to deal with your troubles."

"How did the Larkspur project get started?" Peter asked.

"Most of the important things in the world, from business deals to seductions—maybe even wars—start over drinks somewhere," Gary said. "A group of people waited on the Mayor one day a couple of years back. People who come to see the Mayor come to complain, you understand. These were black people from Harlem. They have their legitimate gripes, you understand. Filthy living conditions, drugs, gangster-controlled rackets, like the numbers, prostitution. The Mayor is a nice guy. He would like to help people who need help. But it all involves money—which he ain't got! Washington these days isn't very interested in helping the big cities; the State Legislature is controlled by upstate small-timers who couldn't care less about us city slickers; the city itself raises every last penny it can through one kind of nuisance tax or another. Not enough.

"So that day the Mayor listened to some pretty impassioned demands from the Harlem delegation. Then he went to lunch with the idea of drinking four martinis just as rapidly as he could. I don't know where he went; the Bankers Club, some place downtown. He found himself with friends—Walter Girard, Ted McCauley, Vince Boswell, some others. He described, in pain I imagine, his morning with the people from Harlem. He pointed out how helpless he was. He muttered something about private capital never doing anything to help. Walter Girard was riding very high about that time, though we didn't know why till a little later. He was courting Elaine and it looked to him as if she was going to say 'yes.' He felt very bighearted. Why shouldn't private capital help, he asked. What did the Mayor have in mind?

"Now the Mayor, like a lot of people today, has the idea that the solution to all problems is a building. Too many people have venereal disease, you build a bigger hospital. The Broadway theater is dying, you build Lincoln Center. You understand, no money to develop new medical techniques for fighting V.D. No theatrical program that has any artistic integrity. Build a building! The Harlem people had a problem. Do they say, let's drive the drug pushers out of town? Do they say let's stop organized crime in its tracks? Do they say let's spend money to improve education and medical services? The Mayor's answer was let's build a great big building, a low-cost housing development. A great, goddamned big building. And Walter Girard, who was feeling like a fifty-five-year-old giant because I guess by then he had Elaine in the hay, announced he could raise the money. That's how it started. Money is power. Money is manhood. Walter would demonstrate that he had the biggest sex organ in the United States by raising gobs of
56

money and capturing the glamor queen of the world at one and the same time. That's how and why it began, Peter."

"I enjoyed the lecture," Peter said, smiling. "Girard raised the money?"

"With help from other bankers, and an enormous amount of small support from the people in Harlem who were sold on the big building idea. With help from me. I'm the best goddamned public relations man in the country if anyone should ask you."

"Sell me Walter Girard," Peter said. "Callahan tells me he didn't need money. Why would he help to steal twenty million dollars?"

"I swear to God I haven't the faintest idea," Gary said. He signaled to the waiter to bring the second round of drinks. "I couldn't believe it when I read your piece, and I couldn't believe it when I heard this morning that he'd blown out his brains. Yesterday, if you'd ask me to sell you Walter, I'd have had no problems."

"Pretend it's yesterday."

Gary drew a deep breath. "I am a woman chaser," he said. "I'm successful at it and I wouldn't trade it for any other recreation in the world. I was called in to promote the fund drive. I met Elaine Summers. They weren't married yet, but it was in the wind. I don't have to tell you what kind of a body she has, you've seen it. I don't have to tell you what kind of energy she has, you've felt it. Perhaps you don't know that under normal conditions she may be the wittiest woman you've ever met. She is full of laughter. She can use some pretty tough language now and then, but it's never just for shock value. It's the funniest way to say something. I took one look at Elaine and I knew I had to have her. Walter didn't bother me. Walter was damn near thirty years older than Elaine. He could never supply that gal's sexual needs, and all you had to do was be

in a room with her for five minutes to know that she exud
the need for sex. She was obviously no virgin, saving herse
for a husband. We looked at each other, Elaine and I, an
I swear we both knew that we could make unbelievab
music together."

"It's Girard I'm interested in," Peter said.

"You have to understand what a great sex king I am
Gary said dryly, "and what a hot dish Elaine is to get
picture of Walter. It never occurred to me that I wouldr
make out with Elaine at once. I was a little surprised th
it didn't happen the first day I met her. Well, it didr
happen then or any other time. I could feel a physical r
sponse to me when I touched her hand, but all I got out o
her was a flat 'no!' For a while I figured she must have
lover stashed away somewhere out of sight. Fifty-five-yea
old Walter didn't have what she needed. I snooped an
spied and there wasn't any lover. And then she and Walt
were married. I asked myself, with some bitterness, wh
this fifty-five-year-old banker, almost old enough to be m
father, had that I didn't have. I saw them almost every da
for a year during the fund drive and at last I came up wi
the answer; came up with it very reluctantly."

"I can't wait to hear," Peter said.

"Mind you, this is the answer I would have given yo
yesterday," Gary said. "What Walter had that I don't hav
was plain, unadulterated, old-fashioned integrity." Ga
saw Peter's eyebrows lift and he went on, quickly. '
mean it. He was a completely honest man. He was what I
was, without any act to impress. He let you see him as I
really was and that was it, take it or leave it. He had som
thing else to offer, genuine, unselfish love. He loved Elai
for all the things she is, not just the shape of her breas
the warmth of her flesh. That's old-fashioned too, yo
know. It's so old-fasioned that it's brand-new. Everyo

desired Elaine. He loved her. Yesterday I would have said he was the most honest man I'd ever met; not just honest in a business sense, but honest in the sense that there were no pretenses, nothing remotely fake about him. Whatever Elaine's life may have been before she met Walter, what he offered her was so unusual, so total, that she repaid him by giving him the same thing."

"And today you would say what?" Peter asked.

"For God sake, man, there's millions of dollars missing and honest Walter blew out his brains. Today I would have to tell you he fooled me with the greatest act of all time."

Peter put down his empty martini glass. "Elaine doesn't think he killed himself. She thinks he was murdered."

Gary nodded. "He sold her such a total bill of goods that she can't be unsold in a hurry. The police don't doubt it's suicide, do they?"

"No. His office, his gun, no strange fingerprints. The motive is obvious."

"To give you a glimpse of what a heel I am," Gary said, "I promise you that after a decent interval of time, when Elaine realizes how badly she was fooled by Walter, I will make love to her until she screams with delight—and for mercy."

"Your sex techniques sound on the violent side," Peter said.

"Total enjoyment," Gary said. "Ready for that cold salmon?"

Peter nodded. "Callahan tells me that Girard didn't need money. Why involve himself in such a risky scheme?"

"I've been asking myself that all morning," Gary said, frowning. "We'll know, when the accountants get through, whether something has happened to his private fortune. I doubt it. Walter wasn't a speculator. You'll find he was in blue chip stocks and bonds and perhaps some gilt-edged first mortgages."

"Why then? Just for the excitement of it?"

"I'd have said Walter got his kicks from being solid."

"So somebody used him in some way, without his knowledge."

"Or had something on him," Gary said. "Blackmailed him into participating."

"Which would mean he was without integrity and he wasn't what you called him—a dead honest man. That may be just what he is, you know. Dead and honest."

Gary smiled. "Elaine really got you to believe, didn't she?"

Was it Elaine who had him wondering, Peter asked himself, or was it Andrew Callahan's offer to get him out of town?

"She knew him better than any of us," he said.

"When a man has a guilty secret nobody knows him," Gary said. "Whatever it was it will come out when the press, and the police, and the District Attorney get through digging. You can't blame Elaine for wanting to keep on believing. But when she stops, get out of my way, brother!"

The picture of Walter Girard, before the exposure of the Larkspur swindle, had been the generally accepted public image of the man. Lehman talked with some humor about the other men on Larkspur's Board of Directors. He had a gift for drawing a sketch of a man in a very few words.

"Vincent Boswell, our Deputy Mayor. Fortyish. Yale. Racquet Club. Oh so veddy, veddy social. Accepted the post in city government because it gave him a sense of importance he had no other way of acquiring. He and the Mayor were both Skull and Bones at Yale, or whatever the most chichi club was. Lightweight. Rich family. I don't know about his own finances. Someone pays his bills, which are constant and large."

"McCauley?" Peter had asked.

"Other side of the tracks, is our Ted. Father came over from Ireland. Bricklayer. Early ward politician. Ted grew up in corner saloon political clubs. He's an operator. Used a lot of muscle, I guess, when he was a young man. Married. Six kids. Got into building. I was surprised when he didn't get the contract for Larkspur."

"How about Edgar Bracket, Larkspur's treasurer?"

"Human computer. An accountant. Started out helping people make their income tax returns on the West Side. Got some good market tips from rich clients. Became Girard's accountant and mathematical genius. Wears glasses an inch thick, goes to mass every day, and I suspect at age fifty is still a virgin."

"And the project director, Lucius Blocker?"

"Big, hearty, jovial man. Out of the Southwest, originally. Texas, I'd guess. Acts like a big, friendly shaggy dog and is sharp as a stiletto. This is the guy who, in theory, had his finger on everything. In theory if anybody wanted to buy an electric light bulb for the men's toilet, Blocker had to okay it. Contractor needs money to buy cement, or steel girders, or what have you, Blocker has to approve."

"So he would have to approve the transfer of money to a Swiss bank account."

"You'll have to talk to someone closer to the operation than I am—that part of the operation," Gary said. "My fees were paid to me by check. The particular account—and I say that because there were probably more than one to cover different phases of the project—the particular account my checks were drawn on was a two-signature account. Edgar Bracket signed them all. Sometimes the other signature was Girard's, sometimes it was Ted McCauley's. I was part of the fund-raising cost. There could be a special account to deal with the expenses of the fund drive, a different one to deal with the contractor, still another to deal with legal expenses. The big sums of money would, you'd think, be in the account used to pay the contractor." Gary grinned at Peter. "One thing I can tell you about all these guys. The living hell is scared out of them right now, guilty or innocent. There isn't much future for any man who just *might* be involved in stealing millions of dollars of public money. You and Elaine have a tough job ahead of you."

"How so?"

"Every one of these guys, guilty or innocent, is going to pray to God that the whole blame rests on Walter Girard. They're not only going to pray, they're going to try to make damn sure that it does."

"And you think?"

"Don't tell Elaine I said so. It might delay my moment of success with her. But I don't see how this could have happened without Walter being aware of it. Your tape confirms that, doesn't it? He opened Swiss bank accounts, your voice said. He would have to know what was going into those accounts, wouldn't he?"

"So your picture of Girard is out of focus?"

"Has to be," Gary said. "He had us all fooled."

"Maybe," Peter said.

"I worry about you," Gary said.

"In what way?"

"You keep believing in Walter you just might get to Elaine before I do," Gary said. "I would resent that, pal. Man, how I would resent it!"

It was nearly four o'clock when Peter found himself back in Jerome Marshall's office downtown. The District Attorney looked as if it had been a long, hard day.

"Any news of Grace?" he asked.

Peter shook his head. He had called his message service when he left the New York A. C. There had been no call from Preston in Washington. "So I don't think I did you much good with Elaine Summers," he said. "I talked some, and she talked some, and I came away half-convinced she may be on the right track."

Marshall looked pained. "It doesn't matter, I guess." He was fiddling with that pipe he seemed rarely to get lighted. "Going through the books and records of Girard's bank may be a long and painful business. He must have burned a bushel of important records. But the police have no doubts whatever about the suicide, Peter. He checked into the office a few minutes before seven o'clock last night. Nobody came to see him." Marshall tapped a thick folder on his desk. "I have a photostat of the sign-in sheet here, and a sworn statement from Whelan, the night guard. Furthermore, it was an unusually light night for after-hours workers in the building. Only four, none of them connected with Girard or his bank, all of them signed in and out, all of them willing to talk quite freely. They can, I'm certain, be crossed off any list of suspects."

"No work crews? No clean-up people?"

"Oh, sure. Clean-up crews work all night. There are a couple of night watchmen who circulate, cover the building from top to bottom about four times a night. One of them saw lights in Girard's office a little after eight. He checked and found Girard working at his desk. No strangers or unaccounted-for people. There's a building engineer who spends the night in the basement where the heating, air-conditioning, and elevator machinery is located. No one out of line there."

"Whelan still could have been bribed to let someone pass him," Peter said.

Marshall pressed the tips of his fingers against tired eyes. "You're pushing for something unreasonable, Peter," he said. "Experts have been over that office. There are no fingerprints there we can't account for. Girard's, his secretary's, a filing clerk's. But the secretary and the filing clerk left the office at five o'clock, the usual quitting time, and both can account for themselves for the rest of the night. No prints on the gun but Girard's. No prints on the metal wastebasket in which papers were burned but Girard's. There isn't one shred of evidence to suggest anything but suicide. There's only Elaine Summers' touching but blind faith in her husband."

"And my hunch," Peter said.

"I'm sorry I sent you to see her," Marshall said. "I warned you she was a modern Circe. I hoped you might persuade her to make a guess on who Girard's associates—the ones he mentioned to her—might be."

"I've had two other contacts since I saw you," Peter said. "At Elaine's suggestion I spent some time with Gary Lehman.

"Engaging young man," Marshall said.

"Engaging and completely bewildered by Girard's behavior."

"Aren't we all?"

"Most honest man he ever knew, Lehman says."

"I would have said the same thing forty-eight hours ago," Marshall said. "But you wouldn't have, Peter. You were prepared to blow the whistle on him. Now that you've done it and he's conceded you were right by killing himself, you begin to believe in him. I find that a little hard to take."

"Bear with me for a little," Peter said. "Tell me about the mechanics of one of these numbered Swiss bank accounts. I used the phrase in my article, but I don't quite know how it works."

Marshall sighed. "I go to Switzerland—or send an agent," he said. "I open an account. I call myself, let us say, John Smith. The account I open has a number. No name attached to it, just a number. When I want to make a deposit I send a check to that number."

"So what's your problem now? The Swiss bank would have a record of your deposits."

"If I could tell them the account number. Any record of that account number that Girard has was probably burned up in that wastebasket."

"But if checks were drawn against the Larkspur Fund the canceled checks would show who drew them."

"Almost certainly burned with the other evidence," Marshall said. "So we don't know what Swiss bank to talk to. We have no records here to help us. Ten-to-one someone has already withdrawn the money from the original Swiss account and deposited it God knows where. All we have from Bracket, the treasurer, and from the accountants, is a preliminary guess that over twenty million dollars is missing from the Larkspur Fund. No canceled checks, no records in the books. The money is just gone. The Police Lab is certain checks were burned in that basket, but there isn't enough left in the ashes to reconstruct."

"Who could have withdrawn the money from Girard's bank?" Peter asked.

"There were three or four separate accounts; a building account, a public relations account, a legal account, an insurance account. They all took two signatures, Bracket's and another. Girard, McCauley, Boswell, Blocker—they could all sign."

"Then Bracket has to be involved!"

Marshall shook his head slowly. "There was, I'm sorry to say, some carelessness. Bracket admits he signed some blank checks on all four accounts. If Blocker needed to pay something quickly on the building end, he had a signed check he could countersign. The others could all countersign. It's not as unsafe a business practice as it sounds. One unexplained check would instantly expose chicanery."

"Why didn't Bracket or someone spot the theft when the canceled checks came in?"

"Because somebody got to them, presumably Girard." Marshall sighed. "Just how it was managed will come out with some hard digging. I've subpoenaed all the people we've mentioned to appear before a special grand jury. They won't be leaving town. Satisfied?"

"No."

"Why not?"

Peter made an impatient gesture. "It's too pat, too clearly Girard. Let's pretend for a minute that he's guilty, Jerry. He must have known at some point the shortage would be discovered. This was not a stupid man. Wouldn't he have handled this so that the finger wouldn't instantly point at him?"

"He'd certainly hope to," Marshall said, frowning. "Otherwise he wouldn't be able to use what he stole."

"So now everything points at him, including his apparent suicide. Suicide is the act of a man who hadn't planned for eventualities. Girard, if guilty, knew he'd have to face the shortage some time. What did the men on my tape say? 'It will certainly be a few months before anybody begins to smell a rat.' So it happened sooner than that. But the other guy asked what they would do when the rat was smelled. 'Then we proceed as planned,' my taped voice says. What Girard seems to have done was not the action of a man who had something planned. It was the action of a man in unexpected panic—or it isn't what it seems to be at all."

Marshall muttered something under his breath.

" 'Proceed as planned,' " Peter quoted from the tape. "Could the plan have been to throw an innocent Walter Girard to the wolves?"

"Your tape says Girard opened two numbered Swiss bank accounts."

"It doesn't say who he opened them for, Jerry. A lot of people have those Swiss bank accounts for tax purpose. Girard could have opened those accounts for a friend, or friends, not having the slightest idea they were to be used in a scheme to defraud Larkspur. Now I blow it with my article, hint that he may have opened Swiss bank accounts in which to hide the stolen money. What does he do? He goes to his wife, declares his innocence, announces that there are 'coincidences' in my story. Could the coincidence be that he had opened Swiss bank accounts for friends? 'I'm going to have it out with some of the pricks who could have done this to me,' he told Elaine. But they proceeded 'as planned.' They got to him, whatever Whelan, the night man, says. They knew he would call them, and they came. They were, laughingly, his friends. They knew he kept a gun in his desk. They slugged him, or held him, stuck the gun in his mouth and pulled the trigger. Then they went through files, records, found the canceled checks and whatever else was incriminating and burned them."

"Those checks wouldn't just have been sitting in the bank," Marshall said. "They'd have been discovered long ago. Girard would have discovered them, Bracket, the bank's computers."

"So what they burned was nothing," Peter said. "They made it look as though Girard had burned papers that would incriminate him. Their plan was to throw Girard to the wolves and live happily ever after on what they'd stolen."

Marshall was silent for a moment. "I can't buy it, Peter," he said. "I'm an officer of the courts, of the law. I have to go by evidence. But it would make fascinating reading."

"You don't mind if I dig?"

"Help yourself," Marshall said.

"I'd like to talk to Whelan, the night man."

Marshall touched the folder on his desk. "His statement and the photostat of the sign-in sheet are there, as I told you."

"I want to talk to him face to face," Peter said. "I want to look at him while he tells his story. He's the key to my theory, you know."

Marshall opened the folder. "Jim Whelan," he said. "He comes to work at six o'clock—about an hour from now. He lives way uptown—154th Street. You'll probably get to him quicker if you wait till he comes on duty."

"Thanks, Jerry. One more question and I'll let you go home to a drink."

"I could use one."

"At Elaine's I met the family lawyer, the lawyer for Girard's investment bank."

"Andy Callahan? I suppose he was Girard's best and closest friend. Damn good lawyer. When I have to face him in court I make damn sure we're well prepared. Does he buy your theory?"

"No. Would you say he was a man inclined toward kindly impulses?"

"Kindly like what?"

"I just met him. I was responsible in a way for his best friend's suicide. I didn't expect a favor from him. He arranged for me to get to Saigon, over the State Department's dead body, to look for Grace."

"That was decent of him. You going?"

"No I'm not," Peter said. "Because I don't think he meant to be kind. I think he wanted to get me out of town and off this story."

68

"Oh, come on, Peter! Why?"

"I think he's afraid I may come up with the truth."

Marshall began to put the top of his desk in order, preparatory to leaving for the day. "There are a hundred people you could find in the next hour, Peter, who would tell you they'd make a better District Attorney for Manhattan than Jerome Marshall. The trouble is none of them really understands what the job requires. This office investigates about seven thousand crimes a year. We eventually convict in about seven and a half or eight percent of those cases. That's a little more than five hundred convictions, a good deal better than one a day. The complainers say that's pathetically few convictions. It happens to be one of the highest rates in the country. Where would we find judges and courts to handle more cases? We make endless deals with defense lawyers—agree to lesser pleas of guilty—so we don't have to go to trial. We are restricted by the law itself. That tape of yours—as you very well know—couldn't be used in court. I know of literally thousands of men guilty of major crimes who are at this moment drinking cocktails in fashionable bars and drawing rooms. Legal technicalities tie my hands. The critics of the way I do my job don't understand one percent of my problems."

Peter smiled. "I weep for you, but what has this fascinating recital got to do with the Girard case?"

"You see, you don't understand why I can't follow your hunches, Peter. But what I was really trying to say is that I am not a journalist and I probably don't understand your problems. So it would be out of order for me to give you advice."

"You don't have to go to court to advise me, Jerry. You know I'll listen."

Marshall stood up. He had gotten his desk very neat.

"You have spent the day," Marshall said, "talking to me

and to a sexy woman who has persuaded you that the facts are not the facts. You are trying to prove her case for her, or disprove it for yourself. If I were you, I'd be following a totally different lead. But then I'm not a journalist and I don't know your problems."

"Stop pretending to be so goddamn modest," Peter said.

"Last night a man you didn't know personally but who had provided you with material for a big story came to see you. It must have been urgent, Peter, because until then he'd kept his identity a secret from you. It was so urgent that he climbed over the back fence to get into your apartment. Your story about Larkspur had appeared in print a few hours earlier. Something had happened that make it imperative for him to get to you. What was it? He tried to reach Nathan Jones, and failing that he came to you himself. What did he have? New evidence on the Larkspur conspiracy? That could have waited an hour or two till he could have reached you or Jones in a normal fashion, couldn't it? *Newviews* is published once a week. You didn't have a deadline to meet last night. But Crown came to see you, prepared to reveal himself as the man who was bugging Tony Larch's office. It was so urgent that he came over the back fence and fell into a trap that got him killed and mutilated. What could be so urgent? I suggest it was danger to you, Peter; danger to you, and to him, and to God knows who else. He provided you, unintentionally, with proof of just how great that danger was by getting himself killed and cut up. Has talking to the lovely Elaine Summers made you forget where your story began, Peter?"

Peter sat still, the memory of Crown's staring, dead face painfully present.

"I asked you earlier if you wanted a permit to carry a gun," Marshall said. "I repeat the question."

You listen to people like Jerome Marshall. He had been

elected and re-elected to his office for a good many years, supported by both political parties. He had come to know his city, and particularly its crime climate, with a thoroughness that was a constant surprise to new people coming into office at times of political change.

Peter cherished his friendship with Marshall. Twice during the day Marshall had warned him that he might be in personal danger. It was time to listen. It hadn't been like any other day in his life. The crushing news about Grace had split him down the middle. He had broken his big story on Larkspur and instead of following it up with all his journalistic skills he had been running like mad simply to keep from anguishing over his own personal tragedy.

He walked through the early twilight from Marshall's office toward the Wall Street area where Girard's office was located. People were disgorging from the buildings, heading for the subway stations and home. Watching impatient, tired faces he wondered how many of them had been hurt by the Larkspur swindle.

For the first time since that moment of horror last night when he had walked into his apartment and found it torn apart and Murray Crown dead in his garden he faced the question Marshall had posed. He had oversimplified it last night. The story had appeared in *Newsview*. Anyone who read it would assume that he had notes, perhaps incriminating documents, perhaps tapes on which he had based his piece. A search of his place was a not unnatural reaction.

But his article had not mentioned Tony Larch's insurance business in Harlem, or the bugged telephone. Crown had to be protected. Crown would be proceeding with his investigation of the narcotics racket. Peter knew that Larch's office phone had been used by someone involved in the Larkspur business; Crown knew it. But Larch, presumably, had no way of knowing that they knew it. Because of the way Crown had been killed and mutilated Maxvil had assumed a "gangland" killing. Because Peter knew that Larch had some sort of connection, at least a friendship with someone, with Larkspur he had assumed it was Larch's men who had searched his apartment and killed Crown. There was no proof of it. Probable but not proved.

Marshall had raised the big question. Why had Crown come to the apartment? Peter's contacts had all been with Nathan Jones. He hadn't even known Crown's name until last night. If Crown had something new to offer on the Larkspur thing, why hadn't he gone to Nathan? He had tried, according to Nathan. He had made several calls while Nathan was unreachable. Why had he come to Peter's? What could he have to tell Peter that wouldn't wait? Why had he climbed the back fence when he couldn't raise anybody with the front doorbell? Marshall suggested he had come to warn Peter of some danger. What danger? It was too late to silence Peter. His story was already on the newsstands.

Peter's mind began to play tricks with him. Could Crown have learned that Walter Girard was innocent and that he was about to be set up for a kill? That would be information that couldn't wait. Crown couldn't reveal himself, couldn't reach Nathan or Peter, and had climbed the wall with the intention of leaving some kind of message that Peter would find.

Peter suddenly had the feeling he'd had earlier that day that he was being watched. He stopped to look in the window of a pipe shop on Barclay Street. The street was too crowded with home-bound people for him to pick out anyone who might be interested in him.

Walter Girard's investment banking business was not set up like an ordinary commercial bank. There were no tellers, no customers cashing checks. It occupied the entire fourteenth floor of the Tompkins Building. The lobby of the building was long and narrow, with a bank of four elevators on each side of it. Like most modern buildings today the elevators were automatic. A uniformed starter was at a standup desk in the center of the lobby. Peter watched him from the street. The man kept looking at his watch. He had arranged a large yellow pad of lined paper on his desk. The exodus from the building was thinning out. There was no attempt made to check out on people who were leaving.

Peter went into the lobby and walked up to the man at the desk.

"Are you Jim Whelan?" he asked.

"I wish I was. If I was I wouldn't be here," the man said.

"Whelan's late?"

"Yeah, he's late. You another reporter?"

Peter nodded.

"You'd think Whelan was some kind of hero, just because he didn't see nobody."

"Is he always on the night shift?"

"Him and I take turns," the man said. "Two weeks night, two weeks day."

"When do you start checking people in and out?" Peter asked.

The man looked at his watch. "Six-thirty," he said. "About ten minutes. But Whelan's supposed to come on at six."

"How does it work—the check in-and-out?"

"After six-thirty we shut off all the elevators but one. No one goes up or comes down without passing this desk. They sign in and when they come down they sign out."

"All night?"

"All night." The man looked at his watch again. "That sonofabitch Whelan is probably out boozing somewhere,

73

telling everybody what a big shot he is. I got a date with a broad at seven o'clock! Whelan might even be trying to make out with that movie star."

Peter's eyes narrowed. "What movie star?"

"What's-her-name, married to Girard. Elaine What's-her-name."

"Summers. She was here looking for Whelan?"

"This afternoon. Some dish! Her boobies are stickin' out there like fruit you'd like to pick. She talked me into givin' her Whelan's address, a rooming house way up town. You think a plush dame like that would shack up with a creep like Whelan?"

"She probably wanted to find out what really happened here last night."

"That's no secret," the man said. "Whelan told it to the cops, to the reporters, to anyone who asked him. First time in his life he was ever important, I guess. No problem about getting him to talk."

No problem, Peter thought, to get him to tell what he'd been paid to tell. If that's the way it was.

"Whelan don't show up here in five minutes there ain't goin' to be nobody on the job here tonight. That broad of mine ain't goin' to wait for me, that's for sure." The man was fuming.

Peter had Whelen's address from Marshall, West 154th Street, way the hell and gone uptown. No telephone. It seemed pointless to go looking for Whelan tonight. The chance that he'd be at home was remote. Peter gave the man on duty a five-dollar bill. "Buy your broad a drink." If Whelan showed up, the man promised to call Peter's message service.

Peter's impulse was to touch base with Elaine. She'd evidently been working at things herself. She'd be at the Warfield Theater where *Glamor Town* was playing. There

74

was no time to get to her before the seven-thirty curtain.

Taxis seemed to have evacuated the downtown section so Peter took a subway to Twenty-third Street and then walked back down and east to his apartment. Mrs. Markell had left things in remarkably good shape. He realized that he was bone-tired. He decided he could lie down for an hour and get uptown to the Warfield to hear the curtain speech Elaine had promised. He checked with his service. Nothing from Washington, nothing from Devery or Nathan Jones or anyone else. For the first time he could remember he carefully locked the French windows leading to the garden. It was just eight o'clock with still remnants of daylight. He set his alarm clock for nine and lay down on his bed. He went out like a light.

The alarm waked him. He freshened up, found himself a taxi at Gramercy Park, and was driven uptown to the Warfield. It was an old theater in the West Forties, standing alone between tall new office buildings. It was a strange piece of architectural elegance out of the nineteenth century, its filigreed stone work balanced by decades of city grime. It was still considered a "lucky house" by people in show business. It had a history of hits unmatched by any other theater in the Broadway area. *Glamor Town*, starring Elaine Summers, had been sold out for months.

Tonight there seemed to be special activity outside the old house. There were crowds on the sidewalk, spilling out onto the street itself. Uniformed cops were guarding the alley-way that led to the stage door and the lobby entrance, preventing people from surging into the theater where the last act of the musical was still in progress.

Peter elbowed his way toward the stage door alley, wondering what was causing the special excitement at this time. He was still some yards from his objective when he saw an old actor friend of his from the Players in the crowd.

"What's all the excitement, Lee?" he asked.

"Oh, hi, Peter," the actor said. "I guess a lot of people had the same idea. I mean, nobody told me about it; I just came. And you see how it is."

"I see, but I don't get it."

"People love that gal in there on the stage," the actor said. "She's one of the few real stars left in the theater today. She's been hit right between the eyes with a big tragedy today, but she's in there, doing her stuff. I wanted to just let her know that I—I loved her, and admired her courage, and was all for her."

"You know her?"

"No, but I guess most of the people out here don't, but they feel the way I do. People are still sentimental in this lousy world, I guess. We owe her something for pleasure received."

Peter edged his way toward the stage door alley. He showed his press card and a special police pass to the cops blocking the way. They seemed good-natured about the situation.

"You're not going to be popular when we pass you through, Mr. Styles," one of them said. "They're liable to kill that little lady with love when she comes out."

Peter walked down the alley, hearing some boos and catcalls behind him. Just inside the iron door at the end of the alley the stage doorman stopped him, fingers to his lips in a signal for silence.

Elaine was singing the soft love ballad that was the hit song of the show. You could almost feel the breathless adoration of the packed house. She came to the last high note, fading it skillfully off, and the audience broke into a thunder of applause.

"You want to see someone?" the doorman shouted over the noise.

"Miss Summers."

"I don't know how you got in, but her dressing room's at the foot of the stairs there. The star dressing room."

The orchestra broke out in a raucous jazz beat. It was the finale, a reprise of all the hit songs in the show. Elaine was belting them out, supported by the chorus. The audience cheered and stamped their feet to the rhythm along with her. And then Peter could hear the machinery of the curtain as it began to lower. The applause was deafening and there were shouts of "Bravo!" The curtain went up and Elaine and the chorus went on singing. Finally the music stopped. The curtain went up and down with no end to the need for the audience to approve. Peter moved slightly so that he could look out through the wings at the stage. Elaine was holding up her hands in a plea for silence. At last they were still.

Her voice sounded ragged with emotion. "I had planned to make a speech tonight," she said. "I wanted to ask for understanding. Understanding for a man who has been falsely accused. Understanding for me. But you—you have given it to me before I asked." She was fighting for control. "I love you!"

Then she turned and ran off stage—and almost directly into Peter's arms.

"Styles!" Tears were streaming down her face. She ran toward her dressing room, but she was holding onto his arm, almost dragging him with her.

She closed the dressing room door. A maid was waiting for her to help her out of her costume. She gave Peter a disapproving look.

"Give me five minutes, Gloria. And don't let anyone else in."

She went over and sat down in front of her dressing table mirror, reaching for a tissue from a box on the table to blot at her tears.

"My God, did you hear them, Styles?"

"I heard," he said. "The love affair is mutual. Did you know there are nearly a thousand people waiting outside the theater to see you?"

She turned to him. "You didn't come here to cheer."

"No, but I cheered."

"Why did you come?"

"I heard you'd been to see Whelan. I haven't been able to find him. Did you talk to him?"

"Couldn't find him," Elaine said. "He never went home after he talked to the police this morning. It's just as I told you. That bastard was paid off and he's split somewhere. Are you beginning to believe me, Styles?"

"Maybe," Peter said. "I've been thinking that—"

He stopped, because the door burst open behind him.

"Gloria, I told you I didn't want anyone—" The look on Elaine's face made Peter turn quickly.

Two men stood inside the door. They were black. Each of them was armed with a submachine gun. Through the open door came the sound of girls screaming and men shouting angrily. One of the men closed the dressing room door, shutting off the sounds.

They were both dressed in black. They both wore black glasses. One of them had an Afro hairdo. The other had a black baseball cap pushed back on his head.

The one with the hairdo spoke in a quiet, quite cultivated voice. "We're sorry to startle you, Miss Summers."

"What the hell is this?" Elaine demanded.

"We're holding you and the rest of your company as hostages, Miss Summers."

"Hostages for what?" Elaine asked. This, Peter thought, was a girl who didn't scare easily.

"Your husband and his business partners stole twenty

78

million dollars or more out of the pockets of our people," the man said. "We're giving them twenty-four hours to put it back. After that, if they don't, we'll start giving them a dead body every half hour."

Outside, somewhere, Peter heard a burst of gunfire.

"Don't be too worried, Miss Summers," the black gunman said. "We're saving you till last." He turned to Peter. "You're Styles, aren't you? I guess you could say we're lucky to find you here. Saves us the trouble of going to find you."

"What do you want of me?" Peter asked.

The man smiled. "Why, you're going to make the deal for us, Styles."

PART TWO
The Siege

CHAPTER 1

THERE WAS A second burst of gunfire from somewhere inside the theater.

"You're holding those chorus girls and the other kids in the show?" Elaine asked. She was angry, not afraid.

"If we're driven to delivering a dead one every half hour, we're going to need quite a few people, Miss Summers. It would be nice if you'd come with me, Styles, without making any trouble." The man with the hairdo smiled, pleasantly enough.

"What's that shooting?" Elaine demanded.

The man patted his submachine gun. "Probably someone's trying to convince someone these aren't toys," he said.

"Do you think you can hold this theater against the city police?" Elaine asked.

"Maybe not, Miss Summers," the man said cheerfully. "But we can kill an awful lot of hostages while they're trying to take it. And I have to tell you that we will if we're driven to it. Will you come with me, Styles?"

"Peter!" For the first time Elaine sounded frightened.

"Where do you want me to go?" Peter asked.

"To talk to Conway," the man said.

"Who is Conway?"

"You might say he's the general," the man said, smiling "He'll spell it out for you."

"This just can't be for real!" Elaine said.

"Oh, it's for real," the man said. "Just as real as all that money that represented so much sweat and toil being siphoned off into private pockets. In all history nobody ever paid back the poor what was stolen from them. This time, I promise you, it's going to happen. Please, Mr Styles."

"Will you send my dresser in to me?" Elaine asked "She's probably scared to death. And I need help to change out of this ridiculous costume."

"If I come across your dresser, ma'am—"

"I can point her out to you," Peter said.

"And will your friend have to stay here while I change my clothes?" Elaine asked.

The man smiled. "Best chance he may ever get, Miss Summers. Now, Mr. Styles, we're wasting valuable time."

Peter look at Elaine. Her eyes were wide, very bright. "I'll get back if I can."

"Man, I don't think you're going to get back," the man said.

Peter walked out the dressing room door into a kind of bedlam. The chorus, the actors, the stagehands, the musicians, even the box office people and the ushers had been crowded onto the Warfield's stage. There must have been twenty black men, all armed with automatic weapons, circling the stage. Some of the girls, still in their very scanty costumes, were crying, some laughing hysterically, one or two shouting obscenities at the gunmen. The male hostages seemed more subdued, as if they were waiting for some sort of cue to action. The gunmen were unmoving black

84

statues, looking deadly efficient.

"This way, Mr. Styles."

Peter's guide made no effort to keep him covered with his gun. It was perfectly obvious there was no way to cut and run. There were more armed men backstage, and Peter had caught a glimpse of others at the rear of the theater. Peter followed his man up a winding iron staircase to a landing that was above the fly-space over the stage. Here were a series of offices, and and Peter was directed into the middle one.

It was a musty, high-ceilinged room with faded velvet drapes at the windows. There was a great, flat-topped Florentine carved desk in the center of the room. A tall, thin black man with a shaved head sat in the highbacked armchair behind the desk. He looked at Peter through gold-rimmed glasses that were only slightly tinted. Looking down at him from the walls were some great ladies of another time. Ada Rehan, Blanche Bates, Mrs. Thomas Whiffin, Nora Bayes, Ethel Barrymore.

The eyes behind the tinted glasses seemed to glitter.

"This is Peter Styles," Peter's guide said. "I was lucky enough to find him with Miss Summers. Saved us some trouble."

"Thanks, Joe," the man at the desk said. He looked at Peter. "My name is Conway."

Peter didn't speak. There was something grotesque about the whole thing. These men were so quiet, so polite, so disciplined.

"I'm in charge of this operation," Conway said. "I would suggest your pulling back one of those drapes and looking down at the street, but it might not be safe. There are probably police snipers in the windows of that hotel across the way. You'd be likely to get a bullet between the eyes."

"I'll take your word for it," Peter said.

"I hope you will, and about a good many other things too, Styles. Let me tell you first what we have going for us. We are about fifty men, all armed with the best modern weapons. We have enough ammunition for those weapons, plus hand grenades, plus other explosive devices, to hold off an army for a month. We have, at present count, seventy-four hostages. Nobody will starve to death in twenty-four hours. That is the number one picture."

Still Peter didn't speak.

"Better than almost anyone else you will understand why we're here," Conway said. "You have been investigating the Larkspur conspiracy. You know how rotten it is. You probably know that literally thousands of black people contributed to the fund. Every dollar they gave hurt. They gave because they were promised something, and, as has been usual down through the centuries, no one intends to keep that promise. I'm sure Joe Robbins told you what we intend to do. We will give them until the close of tomorrow's business day to replace the stolen money in the fund. After that we'll begin to feed them a dead body every half hour—until we run out of bodies."

"I don't believe that," Peter said.

"You better believe it, man." Conway's glasses trembled with his intensity.

"Why have you chosen this place, these people?"

"Because this is the center of the Great White Way. There are bright lights focused on us, Styles. The whole world will pay attention. We take seventy-five people off the street and hold them in a warehouse somewhere, who cares? This is a famous building; these are famous people, some of them loved. You hear that applause tonight?"

"I heard."

"I count on you, Styles, to let the public know why these people are being held. I count on the public to pres-

ire the thieves into returning the money. The public cares
bout Elaine Summers."

"You know who the thieves are?"

"I supposed you know that," Conway said, his voice
iddenly bitter. "I supposed you were saving that for next
veek. Got to sell the magazine, no?"

"I haven't any clear picture of who they are."

"So you've got till the end of the business day tomorrow."

Peter found it hard to breathe. "Just what do you expect
ie to do?"

"You're going to walk out of here a free man," Conway
aid. "Then you're going to have to sell like you never sold
inything in your life before. You've got to convince the
Mayor and the Police Commissioner that we can stand off
iny kind of attack they launch against this building for
quite a while. They come in shooting and hurt any of my
nen we'll toss them a dead hostage out a window. An eye
or an eye, man. You've got to convince them nobody will
get hurt if that money is back in the Larkspur Fund by the
ind of tomorrow's business day. You've got to convince
hem that if it isn't, or we don't have some guarantee from
omeone we can believe, that it will be back, we'll start
eeding them some very dead hostages. You've got to convince them if they try to gas us out or bomb us out, we'll
ust turn our guns on the seventy-four people we're hold-
ng."

"A tall order," Peter said.

"You believe me, don't you?"

"I think I do," Peter said. "I think maybe you're that
crazy."

"Let me make something very clear to you, Styles.
We're not hijackers asking for money to put in our own
ockets. Money has been stolen from people who can't
afford to lose it. We want it returned and used for the

87

purposes for which it was given. It's not good enough for us that the thieves be caught and tried, and put in jail. We want the money back. And I promise you, man, we'll do exactly what we threaten to do if our terms aren't met."

There was something so quiet, so untheatrical about Conway, in spite of the melodrama of his threats, that Peter found himself a believer.

"How do I get back to you if there is bargaining to do?" he asked.

Conway touched the telephone on the desk. "If they have disconnected, make them put it back in service." He picked up the receiver and listened. "Still in service," he said, and put it down. "Write down the number."

"How do I get out?"

"We bullhorn you out," Conway said. He gestured to Joe Robbins, standing silently by the office door. "Let's go on the air, man."

Robbins beckoned to Peter and they went out into the hall and down the winding stair to the stage level. The hostages were still crowded on the stage, surrounded by the silent men with guns. They were quiet now, the quiet of terror.

"We walk up the side aisle," Robbins said. "After we talk to them we let you out through the lobby."

They were halfway up the aisle when Peter heard the amplified voice on a bull horn. He guessed it was Conway.

"Policemen, listen! Policemen, listen! We're sending someone out to talk to you. You hear? We're sending someone out. He'll have his hands up. He's a newspaper man, Peter Styles. You hear? He'll be coming out—right now!"

"Suppose some trigger-happy cop didn't hear?" Peter asked.

"They're your cops, man," Robbins said.

At the rear of the theater there were half a dozen more men armed with rapid-fire weapons. They paused beside he solid doors opening out into the lobby. Robbins appeared to be listening for something.

"Styles is coming out—*now!*" the voice on the bullhorn announced.

Robbins nodded to one of the men who pushed down the ock-bar on one of the heavy doors.

"Give me some time to talk to them out there," Peter said.

"Man, you got till tomorrow afternoon, if you can keep hem from deciding they are heroes."

The man at the door pushed it open and Peter, drawing a deep breath, stepped out into the lobby. The door was closed quickly behind him and he heard the lock-bar fall nto place.

The lobby was dark, no lights on. But Peter could see perfectly well because of the brilliant lights out on the street. Seachlights were focused on the front of the old theater. Through the glass doors at the street entrance Peter could see no signs of life, no movement outside, except the blinking red light on a police car parked in front of the Selwyn Hotel across the way.

He walked slowly toward the glass doors. Conway had mentioned snipers in the upstairs windows of the hotel. Peter's mouth felt dry. If someone up there hadn't heard the announcement from Conway's bull horn, or was too nervously tight on a trigger—

Peter pushed open the nearest door and stepped out onto the sidewalk, under the iron-and-glass canopy that stretched out from the doors to the sidewalk curb. He instantly raised his hands above his head and moved forward. His feet felt as heavy as if they were in diver's boots.

A different voice on a different bull horn came to him.

89

"Styles! Come straight across the street and into the hotel. Around the front end of that police car and into the hotel."

Peter started across the empty street. Up the block toward Sixth Avenue and in the other direction toward Broadway, a hundred yards away in each direction, he saw police barriers had been set up and behind them crowds of people, watching. They were far enough away to be out of view of anyone shooting from the old theater or the hotel opposite it.

Peter walked, with the strange feeling that eyes were boring into him from behind. He reached the police car, circled in front of it, went up the four steps to the front door of the hotel. The minute he opened it he was blasted by the sound of a hundred voices, all shouting and talking at once. Two cops grabbed him, hurled him roughly against the wall.

"Keep your hands up! Face the wall!"

They frisked him for a weapon he didn't have.

"Easy!" An authoritative voice shouted. "That is Peter Styles. Bring him to the office."

Policemen took him by the arms and hustled through a jam of people, all seeming to shout questions at him, and into an office behind the reception desk. The Selwyn was an old fleabag of a hotel, dirt and peeling paint obscuring what must have been elegance fifty years ago.

In the dilapidated office were three men, two in civilian clothes and one in the uniform of a police captain.

"You all right, Mr. Styles?" the Captain asked.

"I guess."

"I'm Captain McGraw, Riot Squad. You know Mr. Boswell, the Deputy Mayor? And this is Sergeant Taylor."

The plain-clothesman nodded.

Gary Lehman had described Vincent Boswell accurately. Fortyish. Veddy, veddy social! He wore a beautifully

90

nade, dark blue, tropical worsted suit with a red handkerchief peeping out of its breast pocket. His face was
handsome but dissipated, and it was ghostly pale in the
harsh light of the office.

"Of course I know who Mr. Styles is," he said. "What
in God's name is going on over there? Do you know that
three policemen have been seriously wounded? How did
you happen to be there?"

"I was waiting backstage to see Elaine Summers when
the curtain went down. I went with her to her dressing
room and a few minutes later two armed men came there
and took charge of us. What happened out here?"

"As soon as the audience was out of the theater they
began firing bursts of machine gun bullets over the heads of
the people," McGraw said. "This area cleaned out in a
hurry. Couple of patrol car cops started to go in to see
what was happening and they were mowed down. Then
they warned us over a bull horn that they were holding
hostages and they'd kill them if we tried to come into
the theater. It's taken us a little while to get organized."

"I was at the theater," Boswell said. "As soon as the
shooting started I ducked across the street and into the hotel
here."

"We'll save time if we let Styles tell us what's going on
in there," McGraw said.

Peter kept his eyes fixed on Boswell. "I saw at least
twenty-five men, all black, all armed with automatic weapons," Peter said. "They've taken the entire company and
the theater staff as hostages. When I left they were herded
on stage. The man in charge in there is named Conway."

"Cleve Conway—black militant!" McGraw said. "They
want money, political prisoners, as they call 'em, released;
the usual?"

"They want the money that was stolen from the Lark-

91

spur Fund returned," Peter said, looking straight at Boswell. "They don't want the money themselves. They want it returned to the fund before the end of tomorrow's business day. If it isn't returned by then, they will start dumping dead bodies out of the Warfield at half-hour intervals."

"You're kidding!" Boswell said.

"I'm telling you what they told me to tell you," Peter said.

"How can the money be returned by then?" Boswell said. He sounded shrill. "We don't know what Girard did with it. It could take weeks, months, before we find it. It could be gone, it could be spent, Christ knows what!"

"Unless you can satisfy them they will start murdering hostages tomorrow afternoon," Peter said.

"You believe that?" McGraw asked.

"Somehow I do. They're not hysterical. I saw no evidence that they were on drugs or hopped up in any fashion. It seems to have been very carefully planned and organized."

"But it's impossible to meet their demands in the time they're giving us," Boswell said. "We'll just have to go in after them, Captain."

"I was told to warn you," Peter said, "that if you start lobbing tear gas into the theater, or you try to rush the place, they'll simply turn their guns on the hostages—all seventy-four of them."

"They wouldn't!" Boswell cried out.

"They might," McGraw said.

"Why did they choose this place, these people?" Boswell asked.

"Oh, that's easy, Mr. Boswell," McGraw said. "The whole world is going to be concerned with what happens to Elaine Summers. These aren't anonymous people held

Latest U.S. Government
tests of all cigarettes
show True is
lower in both
tar and nicotine
than 98% of all other
cigarettes sold.

Think about it.
Shouldn't your next cigarette be True?

Latest U.S. Government tests of all menthol cigarettes show True is lower in both tar and nicotine than 98% of all other menthols sold.

Think about it.
Shouldn't your next cigarette be True?

an anonymous place. You know something? There are people who will raise hell with us if we damage the building. It's a landmark, for God sake. We're going to have to think this one out pretty carefully."

"Get the money back in the Larkspur Fund and you've got no problems," Peter said.

Boswell's laugh was off key. "You got a spare million you'd like to lend us, Styles?"

McGraw wasn't listening. "That's an army in there, not a couple of holdup men."

"Conway told me they have enough ammunition, hand grenades, explosive devices to hold off an army for a month," Peter said.

"How could they get all that stuff into the theater?" Boswell asked.

"It doesn't matter very much how if it's there," McGraw said. "I understand the Mayor is in Colorado Springs at a convention of big-city mayors. I think you better get in touch with him at once, Mr. Boswell. There are decisions that have to be made here, and I don't intend to make 'em."

"May I make a suggestion?" Peter asked.

"Shoot," McGraw said.

"I think Mr. Boswell should call a meeting of the directors of the Larkspur Fund. They may want to make Conway some kind of a counter offer."

"There isn't anything they can do about getting the money back," Boswell said. "That's a matter for the police and the District's Attorney's office, and maybe the FBI if the money's been taken out of the country."

"Isn't it possible," Peter asked, feeling anger beginning to rise in him, "that you and your fellow directors might not want to have the murder of seventy-four people in that theater on your consciences?"

"Oh Jesus!" Boswell said. He looked as if he might suddenly crumple.

"We seem to be sitting on a time bomb here, Mr. Boswell," McGraw said. "Let me get the manager here to put you in a room where you can talk on the phone without being bothered. You'd better get onto the Mayor, but quick. What we do here may go down in history. And Mr. Styles may have something about the Larkspur directors." He signaled to Sergeant Taylor, who had, so far, stood listening. "Find a quiet phone for Mr. Boswell, Ed."

Taylor led Boswell out of the office. Captain McGraw pushed his uniform cap back on his head. "Not the right kind of man to be representing the Mayor in this kind of crisis," he said. "He's great for greeting visiting royalty but not much else. Tell me exactly what the setup is in there, Mr. Styles."

"I didn't see very much, Captain. I was in Elaine Summer's dressing room when these two men broke in. One of them is named Joe Robbins, by the way."

McGraw nodded. "It figures. He's been one of Conway's boys for a long time."

"You sound as though you know Conway."

"I know him," McGraw said, his mouth tightening. "This was a hot city a couple of years back. Conway had his sort of army organized in the black ghettos, here and in Brooklyn. They weren't the ordinary protestors. They helped black people, physically, out of trouble. They shot up a couple of police stations to rescue blacks who'd been arrested—falsely, they claimed. They've staged some pitched battles with organized crime gangs operating in Harlem and the Bedford-Stuyvesant areas. Black vigilantes you could call them. Ask in Harlem and they'll tell you Conway is a black Robin Hood, robbing the rich to help out the poor. We've sometimes looked the other way when they hit someone we knew was robbing the community."

94

blind. Fight Conway and you have the whole black community on your back."

"You can't look the other way tonight," Peter said. "There are seventy-four innocent people in that theater, people who haven't robbed anyone, black or white."

"We're not going to be able to look anywhere except across the street," McGraw said. He'd begun to move restlessly around the room. "You know what's happening right now? The Mayor's office, the Police Commissioner's office, are being flooded with phone calls from righteous citizens demanding that we move in and kill the sonsofbitches! If we can't handle it we should call out the militia—or the marines, for Christ sake. That's what we've got to have, Mr. Styles—law and order! Law and order and to hell with the hostages. It's just tough luck for them, and anyway we ought to be able to save most of them. If we don't go in and we don't save most of the hostages, we should be sent to Devil's Island!" He turned on Peter. "You know more about this Larkspur thing than I do. You're the specialist on it, aren't you? That's why Conway's using you, isn't it?"

"I don't know much more than I wrote in my article, if you read it, Captain."

"Oh, I read it," McGraw said. "The minute it hit the stands we knew we could expect trouble in the black community. And when I heard what happened to Murray Crown—" His anger was beginning to boil. "Did you know this was going to happen, Styles? Is that why you were in the theater tonight? Was it set up in advance you'd do the talking for Conway?"

"Of course not!"

"Nathan Jones is your friend, isn't he? He put you onto this Larkspur thing, didn't he? Just which side are you on, Styles?"

"You want to listen?" Peter asked, his own anger rising

"Okay, I'll listen," McGraw said. "But I'm not in love with anyone who may have set up this blood bath. You know what'll happen the first time they kill one of those hostages and throw him out on the street? We'll go in. A lot of us will get killed, and a lot of them will get killed and God help the hostages."

"I think the District Attorney and Lieutenant Maxvi of Homicide will vouch for me," Peter said. "Yes, I've been involved in trying to expose the Larkspur swindle. Yes Nathan Jones put me onto it. Yes Crown came to my apartment presumably to alert me to something, and was killed by people who were there, tearing my place apart to find evidence I might have on the Larkspur thing. Jerry Marshall suggested I talk to Mrs. Girard this morning—Elaine Summers. She doesn't think her husband committed suicide. I'm inclined to agree with her. I think he was the fall guy for the real criminals. I spent the day trying to get a lead and I went to the theater tonight to see if she had anything new. I never heard of Conway until all hell broke loose in there. When they took me, Robbins said my being there was a stroke of luck. It saved them from looking for me. I think they meant all along to use me as a go-between because they felt they could trust me. Because I knew what had happened to the Larkspur Fund and because Larkspur is what it's all about."

"All right, Mr. Styles," McGraw said. "Let's you and I start over. I've got a hell of a lot of good men in this building, waiting for someone to go haywire across the street. I get real uptight when I think of them being killed for something like this. Can the stolen money be got back into the Larkspur Fund?"

"It amounts to about twenty million dollars, Captain," Peter said.

"God!"

"We think it's been spirited away into numbered Swiss bank accounts. We have no immediate way of locating those accounts. We don't know who did the spiriting."

"Not Girard?"

"I begin to think not, but it doesn't matter. Because we don't have the number of the account or accounts. If we did have, it would take a long legal wrangle to get it back, if it can be gotten back. Certainly not by tomorrow afternoon."

"So we can't meet their conditions," McGraw said.

"Not by getting the stolen money back. Not in time."

"Do you think Conway would accept a promise that when it is found it will be returned to the fund?"

"In the first place it's *if* it is found, Captain. In the second place I don't think Conway will accept any promises. He might give us a little more time—a day, two days. There are at least a hundred people in the Warfield that have to be fed. He isn't going to let go of anyone, because once he does he's lost the ball game."

"Then we can't win!" McGraw said.

"We can't win unless that money is replaced in the fund," Peter said.

"And we don't know where it is!"

"It doesn't have to be that particular money, Captain. The directors of Larkspur might replace it. The city might replace it to prevent a public slaughter. The guilty people might be exposed and their property and other assets attached. What matters to Conway is that the money be replaced in the fund and that it be used to build a building."

"The sonofabitch has some justice on his side," McGraw said.

"It's one in a century-long series of broken promises," Peter said.

McGraw drew a deep breath. "My job is to keep them sealed up in there. But I don't have to go in there after them, and I won't until I get orders from the very top—the Commissioner or the Mayor himself. So I just sit here in command of a force of men. What do you do, Mr. Styles?"

"I try to persuade the directors of Larkspur that they've got to do something," Peter said.

"I wish you luck. You ask a rich man for a million bucks to save a chorus girl he can't lay!"

"By tomorrow morning we may have the whole city bringing pressure to bear on them. Then there's an outside chance of discovering who is really responsible."

"What good would that do?"

"It might lead us to the money. If we knew we could get it back sometime, we might be able to persuade the directors to replace it in the interim. The City or the Federal Government might go for that."

McGraw shook his head slowly. "I've got a hunch you're an optimist, Styles. Do you really think those directors of Larkspur will put up twenty million dollars to save the hostages? Casualties are just numbers today. Forty-six thousand people killed in a war; five thousand in an earthquake; fifty in a fire; three cops in a shootout; those are just numbers, not people. As long as it isn't your wife, or your child, or your parents it's just a number."

"That's why Conway chose these people in this place. Elaine Summers is something more than just a number to the general public."

The office door opened, letting in the clamor of voices outside and a pallid-looking Vincent Boswell.

"I reached the Mayor," he said. "You're to sit tight, Captain, unless they start something from the theater. The Mayor's chartering a plane and he should be here in a few hours. He will have talked to the Police Commissioner by now, so that order will stand for you." He turned to Peter. "The Mayor hopes you may be able to talk reason to Conway, Mr. Styles."

"There's nothing reasonable I can say to him until the trustees of Larkspur meet," Peter said. "Have you called them?"

"I talked to Ted McCauley, the Board Chairman," Boswell said. "He'll try to get a meeting together in the morning."

Peter glanced at his watch. "It's just after midnight, Boswell. They should meet somewhere in the next hour. There are people across the street who may be going to die while they get a good night's sleep. You get them together within the next hour or I'll be on the radio and TV telling the people of this city that you refuse to help the hostages."

"Right on!" McGraw said, under his breath.

"I—I'll do what I can," Boswell said. "Where do you suggest they meet?"

"Here in this hotel," Peter said. "They should get a clear picture of what's going on."

"It's not safe here!"

"It's not safe anywhere for them," Peter said. "Tell them they may very well be Conway's next target if they don't get off their butts and figure out something to do."

Boswell took the red handkerchief out of his pocket and blotted at his face with it. "I'll do what I can," he said, and retreated from the office again.

"He's not used to being talked to like that," McGraw said. He sounded happy. "I figured he'd collapse if anybody took aim at him."

"I want to make two phone calls," Peter said. "First, one to Conway."

"He'll talk on the phone?"

"If it hasn't been disconnected."

"It hasn't."

"Keep it that way." Peter reached for the phone book on the desk and looked up the Warfield's number. He found it and dialed. A smooth voice answered.

"Peter Styles here."

"Hold on."

Then Conway answered. "Well, Mr. Styles?"

"Things are in motion," Peter said. "Captain McGraw who is in charge over here, has instructions not to move unless you do."

"If he cares about the hostages, he better obey those instructions."

"He will. Now listen to me. The directors of Larkspur will be coming here to the hotel to meet. They'll have to come directly into your line of fire."

Conway chuckled. "What a temptation," he said.

"Resist it!"

"You've got till tomorrow afternoon," Conway said. "Unless McGraw's orders are changed. Give him my regards. He's a good cop—for a white cop. Tell him if he's ordered to attack to bring up the rear. I'd hate to be the one to kill him."

Peter put down the phone. "He likes you," he said to McGraw.

"I don't like him," McGraw said. "It's got so I don't like anyone who has a cause any more, or who demonstrates, or who calls cops pigs!"

Peter dialed another number. A husky male voice answered.

"I want to reach Nathan Jones," Peter said. "This is Peter Styles. I'll give you a number where he can reach me."

"Hold on, man. I think he's in his office."

Nathan's office was a booth at the rear end of a saloon in

Harlem. Peter could hear voices and laughter. The saloon was busy. Then a phone booth door closed and Nathan was there.

"You got new problems," he said.

"In spades. Can you come downtown? I need your help."

"You must be kidding," Nathan said.

"You knew this was going to happen?"

"I knew."

"And you didn't do anything to stop it?"

"Man, I couldn't stop the sun from rising in the morning, could I? I couldn't stop anything. No way."

"Will you come downtown?"

"You been listening to the news or watching the TV?"

"I've been making the news," Peter said.

"You haven't been making all the news," Nathan said. "Fifteen minutes ago three perfectly innocent black men were beaten to a pulp in Times Square by a steamed-up crowd. No black man in his right mind will come anywhere near that part of town. I'm in my right mind, man."

"If I come to you, it will have to be later."

"It isn't exactly safe for someone your color up here," Nathan said. "You decide to come up, you call me. I'll have a couple of my boys meet you at the 125th station of the Penn Central. That's as far as a cab will bring you to-night. It's real hot up here."

"I'll call. It may be quite a bit later."

"You making a deal for Conway?"

"I'm going to try to make a deal for the hostages," Peter said.

"I'll tell you one thing, man. Conway isn't bluffing. No way."

With something like shock Peter realized that he hadn't thought about his personal tragedy for nearly three hours.

He called his message service.

Nothing from Washington.

But there was a message. "James Whelan called you just after nine o'clock, Mr. Styles." The night man at the Tompkins Building. He must have called just after Peter had started up town to the Warfield Theater. In any event Whelan wasn't ducking.

"Did he leave a number where I could call him?"

"He said you knew where to find him, Mr. Styles. Mr. Styles?"

"Yes?"

"Are you all right, sir? We've been listening to the radio—"

"I'm fine, doll. Thanks."

Peter dialed the *Newsview* office. He didn't have to be told that Frank Devery would be there. Devery was never out of touch with the minute-to-minute news. As soon as the word was out on the seizure of the Warfield Theater Devery would have hightailed it to his news center.

"Well, boy, you seem to have gotten yourself into the middle of the biggest story of the year," Devery said. "We just got the word here that you're the go-between. Where are you?"

"Selwyn Hotel, just across the street from the theater."

"Are the cops holding up?"

"For the time being. Listen, Frank. The possibilities in this situation are too complex to go into on the phone. Conway's terms are to get the money back into the Larkspur Fund by afternoon tomorrow. Today, actually. The directors of Larkspur are on their way here, I hope. I'll be putting it to them. They may want to raise the money. They may stall until Conway has to show them he means business."

"You think he does?"

"I'm convinced. So is Nathan Jones. So is Captain Mc-Graw, in charge here."

"So the Larkspur boys have to get up the money."

"If they can raise it, and if they feel so inclined." Peter felt a nerve twitch in his cheek. "Pay attention to what I'm saying, Frank. Girard still remains the villian. If I could destroy that myth and point to the really guilty people, it might help. That night man at the Tompkins Building. He called me. I didn't get the call. I want you to get to him, listen to what he says, and judge for yourself if he's lying or telling the truth."

"I can't leave here, Peter. News is breaking every minute."

"So send somebody downtown to get him. Have him brought to your office and talk to him there. I want you, not somebody else, to question him. Was he bought off, or did he leave his post last night—even for five minutes?"

"He's not going to tell me if he was bribed."

"But you can tell if he's lying. I'd count on you any time to see through a lie. He's willing to talk to me, which means he is innocent or he's prepared to make me believe a lie. Work on him, Frank."

"Do my best. How tight are things there?"

"Tight, but under control—unless someone gets hysterical and makes a false move."

The office door opened as Peter put down the phone and two men came in. One of them was Jerry Marshall, the D.A., and the other was Matt Ryan, the Police Commissioner. Ryan was a hard-faced, red-haired, tough customer who had come up through the ranks from a patrolman on the beat to the top spot. The word on him was that he knew the Department inside out, had no use for politicians or influence peddlers. He was a popular man with the cops themselves, a rarity in his job.

103

"You seem to be a magnet for trouble, Peter," Marshall said.

"How did you get involved, Mr. Styles?" Ryan asked.

Peter told his story again.

"How are you deployed, Mac?" Ryan asked Captain McGraw.

"I've got about twenty men here in the hotel," McGraw said, "covering the theater from upstairs windows. Street's blocked off at both ends, as you must have seen when you came in."

"What's at the rear of the theater?" Ryan asked.

"The theater goes straight through to the next street," McGraw said. "Big loading doors back there to get scenery, furniture, that sort of thing in and out. We've blocked off that street too, and I have another twenty men located in the building across the street."

"Equipment?"

"I have two armored cars, one on each street, ready to move in. Tear gas guns ready. The Mayor has relayed orders to me to—"

"I've talked to the Mayor," Ryan said. "I go along with him. He should be here before morning. Suppose they get impatient inside the theater? Suppose their demands aren't satisfied by the deadline?"

"Mr. Styles saw at least twenty-five men armed with automatic weapons. There may be more."

"And seventy-four hostages," Marshall said softly.

"They told Styles they have grenades and explosives— some kind of bombs, I suppose."

"Conway said he could hold off an army for a month," Peter said.

"But if trouble starts now?" Ryan persisted.

"I've sent for bulletproof vests and helmets," McGraw said. "We've got a few here but not enough. If we have to

104

go in, Commissioner, we go in."

Ryan looked at Peter. "What chance do we have of satisfying Conway?"

Peter shrugged. "The directors of Larkspur are on their way here now. They may or may not be willing—or able—to put up the money to save the hostages. If they won't, or can't, then it will be up to the City, or the State, or the Federal Government."

"Twenty million dollars?"

"Thereabouts."

"Who the hell are all those people out in the lobby?" Ryan asked.

"People who were in the theater took cover here when the shooting started," McGraw said. "Others sifted in the back way before we got it shut off—sightseers, relatives, friends, reporters." McGraw smiled a sour smile. "We got enough advice out there on how to handle this to last us a lifetime."

"Where are the Larkspur directors meeting?"

"Private dining room on the main floor," McGraw said. "This ain't the Waldorf, but there's a big-enough room back there to handle it."

"I'd like to sit in," Ryan said. "Somebody should make it clear to them just what kind of a fight we're facing."

"What kind of a fight are we facing?" Marshall asked.

The Commissioner made an impatient gesture. "We start to move in and the ifs, ands, and buts are all over. Conway will not want to be hampered by his hostages so he'll line them up on stage and—pow! Then he'll devote his attention to us. We can't use many more men than he's got." Ryan's face hardened. "Our only advantage is we can bring in reinforcements. When our guys get killed we can move in other guys to get killed. We have to move across open spaces. He just sits inside and picks us off, for as long as his ammunition holds out."

"Tear gas?" Marshall asked.

"Oh, we use that," Ryan said. "So that, too, spells the end of the hostages. They have a big building to maneuver in. There are cellars and subcellars. For all I know Conway may already know of a way out. So we finally walk in and—and bury the dead." He shook himself like a dog coming out of water. "Then they hang us from a lamppost in Times Square for endangering the hostages—not saving them."

"Is there a way to save them, Commissioner," Peter asked, "if Conway isn't satisfied and he throws the first dead one out on the street for us to see?"

"Only God has the answer to that," Ryan said, "because only God knows what is going on inside Conway's head."

"It would seem," Marshall said in his quiet voice, "that there is no way to save the hostages except to get up the money."

"That's somebody else's job," Ryan said. "All I can do is make it clear to the Larkspur people that we can't save them with a brilliant rescue." He turned to McGraw. "What about plans for the theater basement?"

"On the way up here from the City Architect's office," McGraw said.

"What about the roof?" Ryan asked.

"No problem about getting on the roof, Commissioner. The buildings on either side of the theater are higher."

"Isn't that a way in?" Marshall asked.

"Look, Mr. Marshall," Ryan said, "we don't have a couple of drug-crazy kids in there. We have a well-disciplined army of twenty-five or more men, armed, prepared. And a couple of them, at least, have machine guns trained on seventy-four hostages. If we make it too tough for them, somebody says 'Now!' and those hostages go down like pins in an alley." He looked at Peter again. "It's up to you

106

to do a sales job on those Larkspur boys, Mr. Styles. Once the hostages are free, dealing with Conway's army is a whole new ball game."

The directors of Larkspur came by twos and threes, directed by the police to the service entrance at the rear of the Selwyn. They came up to the crowded lobby, most of them looking pale and a little frightened. They were instantly swamped by people asking them what they proposed to do. Conway's demands were no secret to anyone by this time. City Councilman Theodore McCauley, Chairman of the Board, had the roughest time. There were parents of some of the chorus girls being held across the street. They were shrill in their demands. McCauley was a politician, skilled in providing answers, but all he could do at this time was to say he hadn't got all the facts. Peter, watching, wondered which of these men, most of them important people in the world of finance, was in on the conspiracy. Behind which worried faces was the truth?

Someone took Peter by the arm, and he turned to find himself facing a haggard-looking Andrew Callahan. The lawyer had been at the bottle again. His eyes were bloodshot.

"Elaine?" he asked.

"She was all right when I was taken away from her," Peter said. "She doesn't frighten easily."

"She's their star attraction, isn't she?" Callahan said.

"Not to the parents of the other kids," Peter said. "Look at that woman over there! Her daughter's in the chorus. That's her star attraction."

"Can Elaine be bought out of the situation?" Callahan asked. "I could raise quite a little cash out of her personal funds and against Walter's estate."

"Conway doesn't want money for himself," Peter said.

107

"He wants money put back in the fund. All of it."

"Is there a rescue plan?"

"If you can think of one, the Police Commissioner would be glad to hear it," Peter said.

"What about troops?"

"Only so many men can go through a revolving door at the same time," Peter said. "There are a dozen ways to take that theater, Callahan, but there's only one way to save Elaine and the other hostages. Replace the money that's been stolen from the fund. You have influence in high places, as you've demonstrated to me. I suggest you spend the next few hours trying to find twenty million bucks!"

Callahan nodded slowly. "I—I'll do what I can," he said. "If—if you have any contact with Elaine, tell her we're with it. You will be going back in there, I suppose, with answers for Conway?"

"Perhaps, if I get the only answer he's interested in hearing."

A harried-looking hotel manager came up to Peter. "I think they're ready for you in the private dining room, Mr. Styles."

"Thanks." Peter looked at Callahan. "You want to hear what the Larkspur directors have to say?"

"I'm afraid I'm not very popular with them," Callahan said. "You see, I was Walter's lawyer. Some of them think I must have known what he was up to. So help me God, I didn't."

Peter edged his way through the crowd in the lobby toward the corridor that led to the private dining room. Just before he reached it he saw Gary Lehman. He was wearing a white dinner jacket with matching batik tie and cummerbund.

"You get around," Lehman said. "You headed for the meeting?"

108

"Yes."

"I was summoned," Gary said. "I'll have to cook up some kind of a statement for them when the meeting is over. Elaine?"

"I hope all right—so far."

"Sonsofbitches," Gary said. "Why do they have to involve innocent people? It's gangster stuff!"

"The men who stole money from Larkspur hurt innocent people."

"Not the woman of my dreams," Gary said.

They sat down both sides of a long narrow table. They looked to Peter as if they had spent their lives attending board meetings. Three or four of them, like Gary Lehman, seemed to have come away from black-tie parties. The rest of them were dressed in varying degrees of casual summer wear. There were roughly thirty of them, Peter saw, some of them looking anxious, caught off base, some of them expressing indignation at what they faced.

Councilman McCauley saw Peter come in the door and beckoned him toward the head of the table. He didn't look cordial.

"I'm Ted McCauley," he said. He didn't offer his hand. "You seemed to have opened a pretty wild can of peas, Mr. Styles."

"The can of peas was opened by the man or men who stole money out of the Larkspur Fund," Peter said.

McCauley's face darkened. This was the man from the other side of the tracks, the bricklayer's son, the man who had fought his way to the top on his own. "If I'd ever dreamed Walter Girard was stealing from us, he wouldn't have had to kill himself. I'd have done it for him." He squared his shoulders. "Vince Boswell tells me you were in the theater tonight; you got the word from Conway?"

"By now the whole city has the word," Peter said. "What I need from you, McCauley, is the message to take back to him."

"Well, let's get this meeting on the road," McCauley said. He moved to the head of the table and pounded on it with a heavy glass ashtray. The rumble of conversation died away. "This emergency meeting of the Board of Directors of Larkspur is called to order. We had all agreed to meet in the morning, but events have changed things."

"Just what is the situation, Ted?" a big man at the far end of the table asked.

McCauley waved at Peter. "This is Peter Styles. I guess you've all heard of him since yesterday." There was uneasy laughter. "He just happened to be in the theater tonight when Conway's black army took over." The implication in McCauley's voice was that it was no accident. "He was let go with a message from Conway."

"So let's hear it!"

"There are seventy-four members of the theater company and staff inside the Warfield, being held at gunpoint," Peter said. "Conway promises to deliver them to us, one by one, dead, if the money that has been stolen from Larkspur isn't replaced by the end of the business day today."

"So he's going to steal from us too," a bitter voice said.

"The money replaced in the fund and used to build the building," Peter said. "If it hasn't been done within the time limit, he will deliver us a dead hostage every half hour until it is done—or until there are no more hostages."

"Is he holding Walt Girard's wife?" a man asked.

"Yes."

"Maybe we could trade her for the rest of the hostages. Some member of Walt's family ought to pay for what he's done to us!"

"If he did anything to you," Peter said.

110

The room was suddenly very quiet, everyone staring at Peter. Standing over by the door Peter saw Jerry Marshall, a faint smile on his lips, and the scowling Police Commissioner.

"It's entirely possible," Peter said, "that Girard was set up by someone else on the inside to take the rap. It's possible that he didn't kill himself. That he was murdered, and the situation made to look like suicide so that there'd be no investigation."

"What kind of horse crap is that?" the big man at the end of the table shouted.

"It doesn't really matter at the moment whether it's true or not," Peter said. "What matters is what's to be done about those hostages across the street. There are thousands of people in this city who are going to feel that you gentlemen, as directors of the Larkspur Fund, should make up its shortage. If you don't, and those people across the street are killed, this isn't going to be a very healthy climate for any of you."

"Just what are we talking about—in money," a distinguished-looking white-haired man asked.

"Edgar?" McCauley said.

Edgar Bracket, Larkspur's treasurer, stood up. He was Gary Lehman's fifty-year-old "virgin." His thick glasses magnified the size of his eyes. He shuffled a handful of papers.

"There hasn't been time to do a complete audit of the fund, gentlemen. Checkbooks and canceled checks are missing, we think destroyed by Girard before he killed himself." The huge eyes turned to Peter and then quickly away. "Other banking records may be gone. We guess the missing amount is in the neighborhood of twenty million dollars—a little one side or the other of that figure."

"And we are expected to replace it?" the white-haired

111

man asked.

Nobody answered his question.

McCauley turned to the Police Commissioner. "Matt, how bad is the situation across the street?"

"There is no way to rescue those hostages if Conway means what he says," Ryan reported.

"And does he mean what he says, or is he just trying to scare us into shelling out?"

"Your guess is as good as mine," Ryan said.

"And your guess is?"

Ryan looked at Peter. "I think he'll do what he says."

The white-haired man turned to the Commissioner. "Who is this Conway who can frighten the whole New York police force?"

"He is a black militant, Mr. Cushing," Ryan said to Ralph Cushing, president of Seaways Oil. "He's a crusader for the rights of his people. The black ghettos are victimized and exploited by organized crime—white gangsters. Conway fights them in all kinds of ways. He obviously feels his people have been victimized by Larkspur. He's never made any idle threats in the past."

"And your department knuckles under to him?" Cushing asked. "Is he one of the black liberationists who've been ambushing cops all over the city?"

"He is not!" Ryan was obviously struggling with his temper. "You get those hostages out of there, Mr. Cushing, and we'll show you how scared we are of Conway."

"You can't bring them out, Commissioner? The hostages?"

"The families of some of those hostages are out there in the lobby, Mr. Cushing. Would you like to ask them if they want us to charge in there. I don't want seventy-four deaths on my conscience. What about you, sir?"

Cushing looked baffled. "Damnedest situation I ever

112

heard of! Where does Conway think we're going to raise twenty million dollars in less than a day?"

A big man wearing a gaudy sport shirt under a seersucker jacket stood up at the far end of the table. "Could I make a suggestion, T.O.?"

"Go ahead, Lucius." This was Lucius Blocker, the project director, Gary Lehman's "big shaggy dog" from Texas. McCauley's attitude toward him was friendly.

"The way I see it, gents," Blocker said, "is everybody who knows anything knows you can't lay your hands on twenty million dollars in hard cash overnight. It's not reasonable to expect it, however we might choose to view this situation. Now, Mr. Styles up yonder"—Blocker grinned at Peter—"Mr. Styles seems to be trusted by this man Conway. I suggest we instruct Mr. Styles to tell Conway it will take a long time, maybe several months, to know for certain just how big a bite Walt Girard took out of our hides. This Conway appears not to want the money for himself. He just wants to get the building built. Is that a fair statement, Mr. Styles?"

"That's what he says."

Blocker spread his big hands and gave the assembled directors a benign smile. "Seems to me we got no problems," he said. "We are obligated to build that building, and I don't imagine there's anyone here who supposes that we aren't going to build." He looked around for agreement, but no one spoke. "I suggest we send Mr. Styles back to see Conway with our promise that the building will be built. That's what he wants. That's what we promise him."

The white-haired Ralph Cushing looked at Peter. "In your opinion, Styles, will Conway accept a promise from us instead of money in the bank?"

"I don't think so," Peter said.

"I didn't assume he would," Cushing said. "Thanks to

you, Styles, half the people of this city already think we've broken promises to our investors."

"It should be easy enough for you to prove that I don't know what I'm talking about," Peter said.

"I wish I thought so," Cushing said. "However, at this moment we have another problem." He looked around the table. His smile had a bitter twist to it. Peter had the feeling that here was an honest man who was beginning to discover that he'd been put behind a very unpleasant eight ball by his partners in a project. "Mr. Styles hasn't done our image any good before the violence of the last twenty-four hours was dreamed of. I heard on the radio that a man was murdered and his tongue cut out in Mr. Styles's back yard. I assume that had something to do with Larkspur, Mr. Styles?"

"I assume it," Peter said.

"Then Walter Girard made it clear by his death that our investors have been robbed blind. That was made clear whether Girard killed himself, or, as Mr. Styles has hinted, he was killed. Now this black hero across the street has made us responsible, whether we like it or not, for the lives of seventy-four people. We can turn our backs on them, as most people turn their backs on strangers who are threatened with violence. We can look the other way. We can walk out of here. It's up to the police to prevent crime. It's not our responsibility. We can't help it if there are mad dogs loose in our town."

"Hear, hear!" somebody said. Peter thought it was the Deputy Mayor. Vincent Boswell was mopping at his face with that red handkerchief.

Cushing looked at Boswell with a kind of contempt. "I don't mind looking bad. I don't care what anyone thinks about me—but me! But there's no reason to look bad just to be stubborn."

"What are you trying to say, Ralph?" McCauley asked.

"The Larkspur Fund is incorporated," Cushing said. "We are its directors, its trustees. As I understand the law the directors are responsible for what happens to the fund's money. If a black woman in Harlem who invested ten dollars brings suit, my understanding is that we, the directors, will have to make good whatever has been stolen. It might take the courts a while to hand down a verdict, but in the end I think I'm going to have put up my share of the loss. So if I'm going to have to make good what someone has stolen from us sooner or later, I choose to do it now—and save those people across the street."

There was a very small murmur of approval from a handful of the directors. Blocker, whose face had gone dark, spoke in a loud voice.

"The trouble with this country is that we're submitting every day to some kind of blackmailers, or hijackers, or muggers on the streets. Jesus Christ, twenty million dollars!"

"So you don't intend to build the building, Blocker?" Cushing asked. "You'll need to find that money to do it, hostages or no hostages. You're suggesting we promise something to Conway we don't intend to deliver?"

"God damn it, Ralph," McCauley exploded, "maybe we do have to find the money, replace it. But we can't do it in a few hours! If Conway won't take a promise from us, there's nothing we can do—saving those people is up to the authorities."

"Maybe someone else would accept a promise from us," an anonymous-looking little man said. "Maybe someone will guarantee the money until we can raise it."

"How many sinking ships have you rescued in your business life, Bruce?" Cushing asked. "I don't think too many people are going to be willing to rescue us." He

115

laughed, and it was bitter. "It's possible, however, some-one just might be willing to rescue those hostages—and us at the same time. Maybe we'll wind up owing Conway a vote of thanks."

"Oh, come off it, Ralph!" McCauley said.

"My last word," Cushing said. "A lot of you accepted directorships in the Larkspur Fund because it was a great charity; to be a part of it made us smell like roses. Now, having been indifferent to how it was managed, we've let ourselves be stolen blind. It took an outsider, a newspaper reporter, to wake us up. But too late. We don't smell like roses any more. We smell like a stopped-up toilet! We let those people across the street die because it hurts us to part with money and we'll stink up the whole world." The white head lowered and he sat, staring down at his folded hands.

A dozen people started to talk at once. McCauley pounded on the table for order. "There isn't time to turn this into a debating society!" he shouted. He turned to Peter. "What chance do you think we've got to get extra time from Conway, Mr. Styles?"

"I guess he has to believe you're not just stalling," Peter said.

"Are you willing to go back in there and talk to him?"

"If I have anything to talk about," Peter said.

"So the Mayor is on his way back from Colorado. We should get straight through to the Governor—to the White House! Somewhere there's help."

There was a sudden wave of sound from the Selwyn's lobby. A cop in a riot helmet appeared in the far doorway, pushing his way toward Commissioner Ryan.

"There's a lot of big-time shooting across the street, Commissioner!" the officer shouted.

The directors of Larkspur began to stampede toward

116

the lobby. Peter, fighting to keep from being swept off his feet, struggled toward the office McGraw had set up as his headquarters. Once out of the private dining room he could hear the chatter of automatic weapons. Something full-scale was under way.

CHAPTER 2

AT THE STREET level the Warfield looked ominously quiet There was no one in sight. The shooting seemed to have subsided. Sergeant Taylor, Captain McGraw's man, was on the telephone when Marshall, the D.A., Peter, and Commissioner Ryan fought their way through the hysterical lobby. McGraw wasn't there.

"What's going on, Sergeant?" Ryan asked.

Taylor covered the phone's mouthpiece with his hand "Action seems to have been on the roof, Commissioner Captain McGraw's gone upstairs to get a report from our guys who can see what's going on. There were half a dozen bursts from automatic weapons." He took his hand off the mouthpiece. "Yeah? You have to be kidding! . . . Well, can tell you no orders for anything like that went out of here. Captain McGraw's in room 1204. Try to reach him there." Taylor put down the phone. His face looked grey

"What is it?" Ryan asked.

"I was talking to Sergeant Gilligan. He's up above on the ninth floor. He has a clear view of the theater roof up there."

"So?"

"Two of our men appeared in the apartment building next door—roof level. They signaled to our men who are watching from here. They used a rescue rope to get across the alley between the apartment building and the theater. They were wearing bulletproof vests and riot helmets. They had submachine guns. Our guys tried to contact them on the walkie-talkie, but they evidently weren't hooked up."

"Who gave them orders to get up there?"

"No one from here, Commissioner. We had the strictest orders not to make any kind of a move, no matter what happened, without direct orders from Captain McGraw. He didn't issue any orders. I know that."

"Some crazy bastards! What did they do?"

"There's some kind of trap door opens up onto the roof," Taylor said. "They pulled it up and started shooting down into the theater."

"Jesus!"

"Their fire was returned from down inside, but they weren't hit—shielded by the open trap, I guess. Then they took off. Went back into the apartment building over the rope."

"You know what the consequences of that may be?" Ryan's voice shook with anger.

"Yes, sir, I know."

"I want to know who gave that order; who took that responsibility. So help me God, when I find out—" He turned to Peter. "You think you could get through to Conway, Styles? Tell him this wasn't an order. Tell him—tell him whatever you can to cool him down."

"I can try," Peter said.

He went to the telephone and dialed the number of the Warfield's private office. The phone rang and rang. No one answered. He finally put down the phone. "No answer at the moment."

The phone rang and Taylor answered. "Oh, yes, Captain." He listened. "Yes, the Commissioner's here—and Mr Marshall and Styles. Yes . . . It doesn't make any sense . . . Yes, I'll tell the Commissioner." He put down the phone. "That was Captain McGraw, sir. The men higher up in this building saw the same thing. Two cops came over the alley on a rope, opened the trap door, and started firing. Got away the same way they came. The Captain's done some checking."

"I should hope!" Ryan said.

"There's no way those two cops could have got in the apartment building except from the next street over—north of here. No one's gone in anywhere from this block. It's been under surveillance from the moment we arrived. The same with Forty-sixth, the block north. No cops went in any building in that block. The Captain's been in two-way radio contact with the officers in charge. No orders were given to go in. Not a single man assigned to Forty-sixth Street is unaccounted for. The Captain's checking out the men assigned to this block and Forty-fourth Street."

"Two trigger-happy jerks took it on themselves," Ryan said.

"That's hard to believe, Commissioner," Taylor said. "unless they got orders from someone. The general order was that no one should take any action of any kind without a direct word from Captain McGraw. He didn't give any word. I've been with him right from the start."

The telephone rang again and Taylor answered it. He seemed to go tense. His eyes turned to Peter.

"For you, Styles," he said. "From over there." He held out the phone.

"Styles here."

Conway's voice came over the line, shaken with anger. "You can tell McGraw from me that wasn't a very smart move," he said.

"There were no orders given to attack," Peter said. "We're trying to find out how it happened."

"You may have saved us some trouble," Conway said. "Those bastards fired right down onto the stage. Half a dozen people were hit, including one of my men. He's in pretty bad shape. So are two of the girls in the chorus. We may be tossing them out to you pretty soon."

"I give you my word those men weren't following orders," Peter said. "How about getting a doctor in to you?"

"How about it?" Conway said, in a flat voice.

Peter was looking at the Commissioner. "I think we could find a doctor who would go in."

Ryan nodded. "Let me talk to him."

"The Commissioner wants to talk to you, Conway."

"I'm talking to you and no one else," Conway said. "I halfway trust you. I don't trust any of the rest of them. My man has his shoulder damn near shot away. Bleeding bad. One girl got it in the chest. I don't think she's going to make it. The second one got it right in the belly button. There are three others got just flesh wounds. A doctor might give the first three something so they'd stop screaming."

"We'll find a doctor right away. How does he go in?"

"Right across the street from the front door of your hotel into the lobby. He'll be covered every step of the way. If McGraw has any new tricks—"

"No tricks," Peter said. "Hold on." He covered the mouthpiece and explained the situation to Ryan. The Commissioner gave Taylor instructions to locate a doctor who would go in. "When the doctor is ready we'll call you," he told Conway.

"It better be quick if it's going to do any good," Conway said.

"Listen to me," Peter said. "The directors of Larkspur are here. They were discussing ways and means when the shooting started. They need time."

"They have till the end of the business day."

"It may take longer."

"I'll have to believe they're really trying," Conway said.

"You're going to have to talk to someone beside me," Peter said, "because I may not be here."

"Where will you be?"

"I'm going to be trying to find answers that may change some minds here," Peter said. "Hopefully, they may change your mind."

Conway's laugh was mirthless. "I might give you one live hostage for the names of the people who killed Murray Crown." He hesitated and Peter heard someone at Conway's end cry out in pain. "Get that doctor here, Styles!"

The phone clicked off.

Captain McGraw came back into the room as Peter put the instrument down. "There something crazy about this," he said. He looked around. "Where's Taylor?"

"They need a doctor in there," Ryan said. "The Sergeant's gone to try to dig one up for us."

"I've acounted for every man on duty here," McGraw said, sounding like a man arguing with himself. "Every one of 'em was where he should be, accounted for by someone else. I could swear not one of them could have been up there on the roof. Yet there were two men there with complete riot equipment. They signaled to our men in sniper positions to hold up. Our men were surprised to see them because they hadn't been forewarned, but they never doubted they were our people."

"No way to identify?" Ryan asked.

"Not in those riot helmets," McGraw said.

"A couple of super-heroes just out of the district somewhere?" Ryan asked.

"We're checking," McGraw said. "But I've got a cockeyed feeling those two guys weren't cops at all."

"That doesn't make sense!" Ryan said.

"Maybe it does," Peter said. It had begun to fall into place for him. "Conway warned us in the beginning that if the police attacked he would wipe out the hostages. That wasn't any secret. It's been shouted around the lobby of this hotel for the last three hours. Play it cool, or Conway will start a massacre."

"Why would anyone want that to happen?" Marshall asked. The D.A. sounded like a teacher prompting a prize pupil. A smile played at the corners of his mouth, as if he knew what Peter was thinking.

"The result of Conway's wiping out the hostages?" Peter said. "The police go in, there is a bloody battle, and in the end what's left of Conway and his army is destroyed. A few dead cops will get posthumous medals and citations. The families of the seventy-four hostages will bury their dead and mourn them. Someone will bring a suit against the city and lose it. There will also be another immediate result. The directors of the Larkspur Fund will not have to get up twenty million dollars in the next twelve hours. The heat will be off them for the time being."

"Are you saying you think someone in the Larkspur outfit deliberately tried to set up a battle between us and Conway?" Ryan asked.

"To save as much of twenty million dollars as they can," Peter said.

"But we know who stole the money," Ryan said. He

123

looked at Marshall. "Don't we, Jerry?"

"My office, going on preliminary reports from your experts, Matt, has assumed the theft was engineered by Walter Girard," the District Attorney said. "That is to say, we have assumed that Girard committed suicide, which would seem to be a confession. But Styles has additional evidence, a part of his investigation as a reporter. There is in existence, Matt, the tape of a telephone conversation. It's from an unidentfied voice to someone named 'Tom.' This taped conversation indicates that Girard set up Swiss bank accounts; that the money will be 'transferred' in a few days. That tape was made about three weeks ago. It goes on to say that when somebody 'smells a rat' they will 'proceed as planned.' Peter hasn't been able to identify the two voices on the tape. But he thinks—and I tend to agree with him—that Girard may have been framed, set up. If we accept Girard as a self-confessed swindler, the real conspirators could go free and clear."

"If an all-out war starts here between the police and Conway," Peter said, "it would take the immediate pressure off the Larkspur directors to get up the money quickly. It also might divert me from trying to prove my theory that Girard is innocent and attempting to identify those two voices on the tape."

"Who knows about your theory, Styles, besides the District Attorney?" Ryan asked.

Peter was thinking about Andrew Callahan. "I think someone on the inside knows. There has already been one rather skillful attempt to get me to drop the story and leave town."

"You think you have any chance of proving your theory before Conway's deadline?" Ryan asked.

"I can try," Peter said. "I'll need help."

"What kind of help?"

124

"You know about the Crown murder at my place last night, Commissioner. It ties in. Crown produced my tape. I'd like it if Lieutenant Maxvil, who's on the Crown case, could work along with me."

Ryan looked at Marshall.

"I recommend it, Matt," Marshall said.

"I'll try to contact him," Ryan said, and started for the phone.

At that moment Sergeant Taylor came back into the office. With him was a sleepy-looking unshaven young man carrying a doctor's bag.

"This is Dr. George Lundberg, Commissioner," the Sergeant said. "He has an office here in the hotel. He's willing to go in."

Ryan scowled at the doctor. The young man looked as if he'd been on some kind of binge. "You had any experience with gunshot wounds, Doctor?" he asked.

"I interned at City Hospital," Lundberg said. "The bulk of my medical experience has been treating gunshot wounds, stab wounds, and whores for gonorrhea. This is Fun City, you know, Commissioner."

"You know how dangerous it may be?" Ryan asked. "You may be caught in the middle. They may turn you loose after you've treated the injured people. They may keep you there."

Lundberg grinned. "I've always wanted to meet Elaine Summers," he said. "Seriously, a little excitement might keep me from dying of boredom, Commissioner. I'm quite competent to deal with the people who're hurt. I may find I need things I haven't got." He tapped his black bag.

Ryan looked at Peter. "Get on to Conway," he said.

A moment later Peter had Conway on the phone. "A doctor is ready to come across to you," Peter said.

"Tell him not to stop for a short beer," Conway said.

"He's badly needed here."

"He'll come straight across the street to the lobby. Right?"

"Now," Conway said.

"He may need equipment he hasn't got with him. There'll be someone on this end to take a call; either Captain Mc-Graw or Sergeant Taylor."

"Where the hell are you going?"

"To find out who killed Crown and why—on the theory that the same person or persons killed Walter Girard."

"So that's how you figure," Conway said. "I don't think you've got time, friend. Now get that doctor over here, quick."

Peter put down the phone. "You're to walk across the street and into the theater lobby, Doctor. I don't think you have to worry about getting there. They sound urgent."

"So let's go," Lundberg said.

It was an eerie sight, watching the young doctor move out onto the street. There wasn't a soul in sight, but searchlights made the area brighter than day. You knew that dozens of invisible policemen were watching from upper windows, guns at the ready, and that other men with guns were watching from inside the theater, never convinced that there might not be some kind of doublecross at the hands of the enemy. The police were the enemy.

Lundberg moved, almost jauntily, around the parked police car in front of the Selwyn and out into the open street. From a distance voices were raised in what might be a cheer or a jeer. There were still crowds jammed behind the police barriers at either end of the block. They shouted at the lone figure entering the theater, not knowing who he was or why he was going in. He represented action to the people who had been standing there for hours, waiting for something to happen.

126

At the doors to the lobby Lundberg turned and faced the hotel. He waved at whoever might be watching, and then disappeared into the dark lobby. At the far end of it a door would open and swallow him up. When he was gone the people in the hotel lobby began to cheer.

"That may be as safe as taking a morning shower compared to what I think you have in mind, chum," Marshall said at Peter's elbow.

"I'm going to see Nathan Jones. That should be safe enough," Peter said.

"You're going after Tony Larch and his boys," Marshall said.

"Someone had access to his phone; someone connected with Larkspur; someone who called 'Tom.'"

"And someone stripped your apartment and murdered Crown in gangland style." Marshall's smile was thin. "I ought to place you in protective custody. You still think Andrew Callahan was trying to get you out of town for criminal reasons and not just to do you a pleasant favor?"

Peter nodded. "He knew Elaine had persuaded me to investigate the possibility of Girard's innocence. Instantly he offered me what he thought was a sure way to make me forget the whole affair."

"I find it hard to believe about Andy Callahan," Marshall said. "And yet I'll tell you an axiom in my business. Whenever there is a big-league crime, like the Larkspur business, or any kind of syndicate operation, we look for a lawyer."

"Because—?"

"Big-time criminals need to be sure they don't get hung up on legal technicalities they haven't thought of. The old-time prohibition gangsters, the modern organized-crime boys, hiding behind legitimate business fronts, are caught for income tax frauds or evasions rather than the crimes we think they committed. The big-shot lawyer saves them

127

from that kind of mistake, from failing to fill out some business form, from all kinds of technicalities they don't dream
exist. The lawyers for these guys get fat and rich, keeping
them from making small mistakes. That's why we always
look for the lawyer. Andrew might be—could be—" Man
shall let it lie there.

Peter was escorted by a cop out the back entrance of the
Selwyn and down to the Broadway barrier at the end of the
street. He had literally to fight his way through the crowd
there, people clamoring to know what was going on. His
intention was to get to a telephone, but several people from
the crowd kept clinging to him, asking him questions, walking along with him. He must be important; he'd been
brought out by the police. Finally he managed to flag a taxi.
He told the driver he wanted to go to the 125th Street station of the Penn Central.

"But I want to stop somewhere there's a pay phone."

"If I was you I'd take my train from down here," the
driver said. "Things are boiling uptown. I ain't too anxious
to drive up there myself, to tell you the truth."

"I'm not taking a train," Peter said. "I'm meeting someone there. Just get me to a telephone."

The driver headed east on Forty-eighth Street and
stopped at a sidewalk booth on Madison Avenue. Peter
called Devery.

"I talked to your man Whelan," Devery said.

"Well?"

"Oh, he's a real chummy guy," Devery said. "Willing to
sing all night, but always the same tune. He never left his
post. No one came to see Girard. He didn't have to go to
the john, no less! There's nothing wrong with his bladder."

"And you think—?"

"I'd bet a year's profits he's lying up a storm," Devery

aid. "It's just a hunch, you understand. But he says the same words, over and over, as if he'd learned them by heart."

"He's gone back on the job?"

"What else? If he splits, everyone will know he's lying. I told him if he'd come back sometime tomorrow we'd take his picture, print it in the magazine. He'll come back. I thought you might want to talk to him yourself. Where are you?"

"Only a few blocks from you. I'm on my way uptown to see Nathan Jones."

"You can be walking right into a meat grinder, pal. What's your theory?"

"I think Tony Larch's mob wrecked my apartment and killed Crown. It may sound wild, but I think two of Larch's men posed as cops and tried to start a riot at the Warfield a little while back. Larch has to be a partner in the Larkspur business. He's the only lead I've got. Nathan can, if he will, tell me how to get at him."

"You want me to send flowers, or contribute to your favorite charity—which I take it is a home for one-legged idiots! Leave it to the cops, Peter!"

"Elaine Summers and seventy-three other people are hanging by a thread back there in the Warfield," Peter said. "We've got to smoke somebody out into the open."

He hung up on a steady stream of profanity from Devery. He stood staring at the phone for a moment and then he called his service. No message from Preston in Washington.

He called Nathan and found him at his "office." "I'm at Forty-eighth and Madison. I'm starting uptown now in a cab."

"My boys will be waiting for you at the station," Nathan said. "Don't try coming here by yourself."

129

Peter went back to the cab and they started uptown. They'd only gone a few blocks when the driver half-turned his head. "You hot or something?" he asked.

"Meaning?"

"There's a black Ford Maverick been following us ever since I picked you up. I didn't pay any attention at first. But when I parked by that booth he parked just behind us. He's tailing us now."

Peter looked ahead into the rearview mirror. He could see the headlights of the Maverick staying just a car length or so behind them.

"You say they picked us up back on Broadway, where ·I came through the police lines to hail you?" Peter asked.

"I didn't notice where you came from," the driver said. "But that baby has been with us ever since I took you on."

It didn't make sense, Peter told himself. It must be a coincidence, and the Maverick would presently turn off their trail. But why had they parked when the taxi parked? What didn't make sense was that the Maverick had apparently been waiting for him, and yet nobody had known when he was coming out, or that he was coming out. No one could have known that he would walk west from the Selwyn to Broadway instead of east to Sixth Avenue. It would have been more reasonable for him to have gone to Sixth, since it was one-way headed north, the direction he wanted to go, while Broadway and Seventh Avenue at Times Square were one-way headed south. As a matter of fact he'd suggested to the policeman who escorted him out of the Selwyn that he wanted to go to Sixth, but the cop said he had orders to take everyone the other way.

He suddenly thought he had an answer and he relaxed. Marshall or Ryan were having him covered, protected. The Maverick was probably an unmarked police car with two-way radio or a car telephone. They'd been ready for

130

him because they'd been alerted that he was coming.

"I think it's cops," Peter said to the driver.

"So you are hot!"

"Cops are my friends tonight," Peter said. "I think they're just trying to make sure we don't get into trouble uptown."

"I sure hope you're right," the driver said. "This is an uptight city tonight, man. What's going on back there at the Warfield, and our dispatcher's been warning us for the last two hours not to go north of 110th Street. They say it's ready to explode where you're headed, mister."

The traffic was thin, not abnormal for three in the morning. The Maverick followed at a reasonable distance. There was no chance they could lose the cab. It took about twenty minutes to hit the far end of the Park at 110th Street. There was something a little ominous about the feel of the city after that. There was no traffic at all; nothing but Peter's cab and the trailing Maverick. Most of the houses were dark, only a few scattered lights in a few scattered windows.

The cab driver went straight through to 125th Street and then headed east for the Penn Central station. Strangely, 125th Street, usually a busy area even at this hour of the night, was deserted. A few shop windows were lighted, dummies wearing mod clothes staring blankly out at nothing. Peter began to feel a kind of tension mounting in him.

"Boy, they really pulled in the sidewalks after them," the driver said. "I ain't never seen it like this. Even the bars and food stands are closed. Looks like you could starve to death before you could buy a hamburger and a cup-a tonight. You sure you don't want to head back downtown with me, pal? Because I'm goin', and quick."

The railroad tracks are overhead at the 125th Street station. Waiting room lights showed through grimy windows

131

at the street level. Peter glanced in the rearview mirror again and saw that the Maverick had pulled up half a block behind them. He paid the driver and included a generous tip.

"I hope you know what you're doing, man," the driver said. "Thanks, and I hope I don't read about you in the paper."

"Maybe you will," Peter said. "My name is Styles."

The driver stared at him with his mouth hanging open. "You're the guy who—"

Peter didn't hear the rest of it. He hurried across the sidewalk into the waiting room. In a far corner of the dim, deserted place he saw two familiar figures, Nathan's two giant bodyguards, one in orange, one in green, their baseball caps pulled down over their black glasses. They came toward him.

"Didn't take you too long," the orange one said.

"I found a cab driver who was willing to come all the way," Peter said. "It was safe enough. Cops followed us all the way."

"Cops?"

"Unmarked black Ford Maverick. It's parked just down the block."

"Take a look," Orange said to Green.

The green one moved over to the station door and looked out. He came back after a moment, moving a little more quickly. "Some cops," he said. "I'd know that car anywhere. Know the license number."

"Larch?" the orange one asked.

"Right on, man."

"Why would Larch have me followed?" Peter asked.

"You came up here to look for him, didn't you?" Orange said.

The two black men looked at each other.

"You afraid of rats, Mr. Styles?" Green asked.

"Why?"

"We don't like the feel of it," Orange said. "A white man gets gunned-down up here tonight and nobody's going to ask much about it. It's part of the scene. We're supposed to get you to Nathan in one piece."

"What's that got to do with rats?"

"We don't like the looks of that car," Green said. "We're going to try the back alley route. That's rats and garbage, man. Someone might drop a flower pot on our heads, but that's better than Larch's boys with a chopper."

"You think they're after me, not just trying to find out where I'm going?" Peter asked.

"They know where you're going. What else would you come to Harlem for tonight except to see Nathan? You see that door over there next to the men's room? It opens out onto a side street. About twenty yards down the block, across the street, there's an alley between a warehouse and a garage." Green turned to Orange. "Make sure the door is unlocked."

Orange sauntered across the waiting room as if he was headed for the men's room. In passing he tried the side door. He turned and nodded.

"Now we move real casual, real slow, man," Green said. "You could stop to light up a cigarette if you've got one. We keep talking, like we were talking business, you catch? But when we reach that door we run like hell. I know about your leg, Mr. Styles. You hang onto my belt if you got doubts. Unless we're wrong that car is going to come around the corner real fast, once we move."

"Let's go."

"Casual-like, real casual," Green said. "I could go over to that phone booth and call for help, Styles, but I have the feeling the minute they see me in that booth they'll come right on in here for us."

Peter fumbled in his pocket for a cigarette. His hands weren't quite steady as he lit it. Green, his head bent, kept talking earnestly about nothing Peter could remember later. It was part of a visual act, the words unimportant. Orange actually opened the door to the men's room.

"Now!" Green shouted.

Peter had hold of his belt as they plunged out the side door. The moment they were out in the open he heard the roar of the Maverick's engine and the squeal of tires. The alley across the street seemed miles away. For a moment he thought his legs were going to fly out behind him, like Alice in Wonderland. Green moved like a powerful fullback in an open field.

Peter heard another screeching of tires and caught a glimpse of the black Maverick skidding around the corner to his right, having underpassed the railroad tracks.

"Go, man!" Orange cried out behind Peter.

He could feel Green literally dragging him forward. Then for the third time that night he heard the chattering of an automatic weapon. He saw the brick wall of the building just ahead of him chewed up by lead—and Green was in the alley and dragging him along. Peter heard a little cry of pain from Orange, behind him.

"Keep coming, man!" Green shouted.

Peter let go of Green's belt and turned, gasping for breath. He saw Orange down on his hands and knees. The men in the Maverick were firing into the mouth of the alley, bullets whining as they ricocheted off brick walls. Orange had managed to maneuver himself behind a heavy, overflowing metal trash basket. He had produced a gun and was firing back toward the street.

Green had Peter by the arm, trying to drag him on into the alley.

134

"I think your friend has been hit," Peter said.

"Ollie!" Green shouted.

Orange only half-turned his head. "My leg," he called out. "I can't walk good, but I can shoot off anyone's head who tries comin' thisaway. Get movin', black boy, before they figure how to stop up the other end."

"Do I have to carry you?" Green said to Peter. "Because, by God, I will if I have to. We'll come back for Ollie."

Windows overlooking the alley opened and heads appeared. The gunshots had done it. People shouted down at them but there was no kind of attack. They couldn't run too fast in this narrow space, cluttered with rubbish, paper cartons filled with junk, garbage thrown casually out of windows. Animal life was stirring. Peter saw the rats he'd been promised and a couple of lean, rangy cats that looked like predatory man-eaters.

The machine gun sounds had stopped. There were two sharp reports from a handgun. Someone shouted down at Green from a second-floor window.

"Ollie's got 'em pinned down for now, man."

Green waved a big hand. Peter stumbled after him, lungs bursting. Up ahead the alley seemed to come to an end. A board fence blocked it, rising up a good fifteen feet. In the half dark Peter saw that there was a door in the fence. Green had reached it and was pounding on it. A head peeped out an upstairs window and instantly disappeared. Seconds later the door in the fence opened and Peter saw a giant black man, stripped to the waist, his body glistening with sweat. He had on a white chef's hat and he was holding a glittering meat cleaver in his right hand. When he recognized Green he stood aside and Peter found himself dragged into an oppressively hot kitchen. The chef character closed and bolted the door behind them. Green leaned against a butcher's block on which the chef had obviously

135

been cutting chops off a lamb carcass.

"Where's Ollie?" the chef asked.

"We gotta go get him," Green said. "He got a slug in him." He straightened up. "Come on, Styles. I'm supposed to deliver you to Nathan."

They pushed through a pair of swinging doors and into a place Peter had visited before, coming in the other times from the front entrance. There was a long mahogany bar up front, and a square room at the back partitioned into booths. In spite of the hour the bar was busy.

In a corner booth was Nathan talking with a couple of friends. At the sight of Green and Peter the two strangers drifted away toward the bar.

"Trouble?" Nathan asked. Ceiling lights were reflected in his glasses.

"A mob car—that new black Maverick? Followed Styles from midtown, he says. Ollie and I figured we walk along the open street the three of us might get it. So we come by the alley. I got to go back for Ollie. He stopped a slug."

Nathan raised his hands and put a forefinger in each corner of his mouth. The whistle was piercing. Everyone in the bar turned to look. Nathan made an ear-to-ear throat-cutting gesture. Action was instant. A couple of men went to the street door, closed it and bolted it. Three windows that opened onto a side street were closed, and iron shutters moved into place. The bartenders, two of them, proceeded to produce rifles and handguns from a cabinet and place them on the bar.

"What do you need, Paul?" Nathan asked Green. He hadn't spoke to or even recognized Peter so far.

"It's Ollie's leg, I think," Green said. "Couple of guys to prop him up. Give me one of them choppers and I'll ride shotgun."

"Luke! Lincoln!" Nathan called out. "Paul will tell you

136

what!" The black glasses turned at last toward Peter. "Well, Styles, you seem to be stirring up quite a storm in this man's town tonight."

Peter was leaning against the corner of the booth, still breathing hard. "As I recall, you're the one who asked me to a few weeks back."

CHAPTER 3

NATHAN WAVED TOWARD the front of the armed bar. "Don't want Larch's hoods moving in on us unprepared," he said. "You look like a man who could use a drink."

"I could stand a Jack Daniels on the rocks," Peter said.

"We don't carry that kind of fancy booze," Nathan said. "But I can give you some bourbon that won't poison you. Connie!" The bartender waved to him. "My special on the rocks. One double, one single. Sit down, Styles, I don't want you caving in on me."

Peter slid into the booth. "You figured Larch was after me?" he asked. "Is that why you sent your boys to meet me?"

"Wrong," Nathan said. "I thought any strange white man walking our streets tonight might run into trouble. Why do you think Larch is after you, man?"

"Maybe because I talk too much," Peter said, with a touch of bitterness. "I've made it clear to too many people that I don't think Walter Girard killed himself. I think he was murdered. I'm trying to find proof. I'm trying to find it in a hurry. It might be a way to break the deadlock downtown."

"You got any leads that hold water?"

138

"I've got Jerry Marshall half-believing," Peter said. "The only person I can put a name to is Andrew Callahan. Only because he tried to get me out of town." Peter elaborated on that. The bartender brought the drinks.

"Just why did you want to see me?" Nathan asked. The black glasses made his face a blank.

"Why did Crown come to see me yesterday, Nathan? Why did he come over the fence into my back yard where he was trapped? You said he'd been trying to reach you. Why?"

"I told you I don't know why."

"You'll tell me what you want to tell me."

"Easy, man. I really don't know what had Crown stirred up."

"He wouldn't have come to me unless it had something to do with Larkspur," Peter said. "I wasn't connected to or concerned with his attempt to nail Larch on a narcotics charge. It had to be Larkspur."

"Reasonable," Nathan said.

"So he'd learned something new. Did it come over that tapped phone? If so, where did he keep his tapes?"

Nathan was silent. He took time to go through the rather elaborate routine of lighting a thin, black cigar. "I had no idea where he was living," he said, finally. "He was playing the whole game very close to the vest. He didn't tell me or anyone else how he was working things. Oh, he trusted me, Styles. But under certain conditions almost any man can be made to talk. Safest thing was not to tell anyone anything. But last night, after he was dead, I sent out the word. I wanted to know where he was living. I got an answer. I went there with Paul and Ollie—a small room over a grocery store, not far from here. We were too late."

"How do you mean?"

"It had been torn apart, like your place. If he kept any-
139

thing there, it was gone."

"Would he have kept the tapes there, do you think?"

Nathan flicked the ash off his cigar. "You're dealing with a fairy tale, Styles. You've invented a theory and you're trying to prove it."

"But I—"

"Easy, man. I've invented a theory too. I wonder how many places it will touch base with yours. Care to hear it?"

"I care."

Nathan turned the cigar around in his fingers, studying it. "Crown wouldn't have been so anxious to reach me, and obviously so anxious to reach you when I turned up missing, unless it was urgent. He could have waited until one of us could be reached by phone. He wanted us to know something before it was too late."

"Too late for what?"

Nathan shrugged. "Too late to stop it, maybe? He couldn't show in the picture without risking his own life."

"He did risk it."

"I don't think so," Nathan said. "He couldn't have known there were people in your apartment when he tried to get into it to leave you a message. If he'd known, he wouldn't have gone in, or he'd have gone in prepared. He was a very tough operator."

"So what could have been so urgent?"

"Something that came over that tapped phone line," Nathan said. "That was Wednesday. Your article appeared that morning. The Larkspur thieves, whoever they are, were caught unprepared. They had to 'proceed as planned,' right?"

Peter nodded.

"Whatever that plan was it hadn't included you. They had to know that sooner or later accountants and auditors would turn up the theft from the fund. But, if we're to

140

believe the tape, they thought that was a few months off. You made it right now. You hadn't been part of the plan. First thing they had to do was search your place to find any evidence you might have. While they're searching, in comes Crown, caught way off base. I think we can take that much of it as fact."

"Go ahead."

"Now comes my fairy story, man. When your piece appeared there must have been some pretty hysterical guys around. They had to get in touch with each other. Someone used Larch's tapped phone. Someone revealed part of the 'plan.' Crown heard it." Nathan studied the end of his cigar again. "Could it be, Styles, that Crown heard on the phone that Girard was to be set up for a hit—a fake suicide? That fake suicide would cover everybody's tracks. Someone had to sucker Girard to his office, and there had to be a hit man there to kill him and make it look like he killed himself and burned the evidence. The hit man would be Larch or one of his boys. Still fairy story, you understand, but I don't think they'd trust that job to a hundred-dollar hatchet man. I'm guessing Larch was in on the main deal. I'm guessing he took on the job himself."

"No proof at all," Peter said.

"I know. I told you, fairy story. Now Crown, if he heard this on his tapped line, couldn't go to the cops, couldn't go to any public person without revealing himself and what he was up to. Revealed, he was a dead man. The only people he could trust were me and you. He could trust me, because he knew me. He could trust you because I trusted you and because, as a newspaper man, you didn't have to reveal your sources. You could warn Girard, the District Attorney, without telling them how you knew what you were telling them. So failing to reach me, he came over your back yard fence." Nathan sighed, and put

141

his cigar down in the ashtray on the table. "Larch himself may have been in your apartment. Maybe just one of his trusted men was in charge. But the minute Larch or his man saw Murray Crown they didn't have to be geniuses to guess that he'd been the source of the facts in your article. They killed him and left his mouth empty as a warning to other people who might talk. Larch has his eyes and ears in this part of town too, you know. They found out where Crown was living and ripped his place apart."

"Why?"

"Everyone who knew Crown and his history as a cop knew he was an electronics expert. I'll bet you another drink that the first thing Larch did was to check his office phone and found it was bugged. But if he didn't find tapes in Crown's room, he has to be thinking that you have them or know where they are. And he must have known that there was dangerous talk over that phone that morning, after your article appeared. That's why they're after you, man."

"I wouldn't be much good to them dead," Peter said.

"I don't think they meant to kill you—yet," Nathan said dryly. "That's why they followed you from downtown. They could have grabbed you off any time along the way. They hoped you would lead them to where Crown kept the tapes hidden. They let you go into the station. Tapes might be in a locker there? When they saw my men and you started to run they tried to make you stop. Next step would be direct pressure on you; make you talk."

"Those weren't warning shots they fired at us. Your man Ollie was hit."

Nathan picked up his cigar and relit it. "You fire a sub-machine gun into a narrow alley and the slugs bounce around like dice in a cup. Ricochet. They wanted you to stop. They'd hoped you'd take them to the tapes. When

142

y saw you with my boys they knew they'd lose you.
ey can't afford to let you get those tapes to the honest
mbers of the Larkspur Board."

'I wish I could. I wish to God I knew where they were.
I had them I might be able to bail out Elaine and those
er people in the theater."

"Well, if there's any truth in my fairy tale we know
ere they aren't."

"Oh?"

"Larch hasn't got them, and he wants them real bad, man.
he doesn't find them, they could cost him his share of
enty million dollars."

The swinging doors from the kitchen swung open and
lie, the big man in the orange shirt, came in, supported
both sides by the two men who'd gone with Paul, the
een shirt, to get him. Paul brought up the rear. Ollie, his
is draped over his supporters' shoulders, grinned at
than.

"Right through the calf of the leg," he said. "I don't
nk it even grazed a bone. Just kind of paralyzed me for
ell."

"Doc's up front," Nathan said. "Have him look at it. You
nk they were trying to bring you down, Ollie?"

"No way, man. They could have sawed me in half if
y'd wanted to. I was like the rear guard. Goddamn bul-
bounced off the wall, the way I figure."

"Get yourself fixed," Nathan said.

"Right on," Ollie said, and was helped toward the front
the bar.

Paul, his green shirt dark with sweat, came over to the
oth. "It was a ricochet, no question," he said. "All the
ots they fired hit two or three feet over our heads."

"The Maverick?" Nathan asked.

"Long gone, man."

143

"See if Doc needs anything for Ollie. And thanks, Paul

"No sweat, man."

Paul headed toward the group who were congregate
around Ollie at the bar.

"Two good boys," Nathan said. The flame from h
lighter reflected in the black glasses as he got his cig
going again. "We got to be right about this, Styles. Ho
come they were able to pick you up so easy downtown?

Peter took a sip of his drink. The cop at the Selwy
had made him go to Broadway instead of Sixth Avenu
which would have been more convenient. It was routine, a
order that covered everyone who left the Selwyn by th
back way. The Selwyn was crawling with people wh
could be involved in the Larkspur conspiracy. He had dor
too much talking. Any one of the conspirators could hav
been aware he planned to leave. The black Maverick an
its gunmen were waiting where they knew Peter woul
have to emerge, either by careful arrangement or becau:
they knew what the routine orders were.

Peter spread it out for Nathan.

"They were waiting for you, all right," Nathan sai
"There's no question in my mind they hoped you woul
lead them to the tapes."

"Why would they think I didn't have them already?"

"If you'd had them, man, you'd have played them fo
that directors' meeting. Or you'd have quoted what was i
them. You didn't, so you still haven't got them. But the
figure you'll know where to look."

Peter finished his drink. "So what in hell is the nex
move, Nathan?" He glanced at his watch. "Time is closin
in on those people in the Warfield. Eleven hours left whil
we sit here with our theories."

"You're not going to be able to go anywhere or do any
thing without Larch on your tail," Nathan said. "Ten t

one his boys are out front, and out back."

"It's ironic," Peter said, "because I don't know where to go or what to do. I counted on you to steer me."

"I knew that's why you were coming," Nathan said. "I arranged for you to talk to someone who might help. She should show up any minute now."

"She?"

"Crown's woman," Nathan said. "Not easy to get her here. Larch's boys have been looking for her. She's been hiding out since the news about Crown broke. They'd try to make her talk whether she knows anything or not."

"Will she talk to you?"

Nathan smiled. "I count on you to be persuasive, man," he said. His black glasses looked up toward the ceiling. "We're bringing her in over the roof tops." He looked back at Peter. "Another drink?"

Peter shook his head. A kind of aching fatigue had set in. The odds against him as one man fighting the conspiracy were rough. He had to convince Marshall, he had to get the police working on his side instead of concentrating on Conway, holed up in the Warfield with his hostages. The honest members of Larkspur's Board had to be persuaded that the villains were sitting at the same table with them; that Girard was not their answer. Without the tapes, how could they be convinced in time?

"Conway's made this ten times harder," he said to Nathan. "He's put a time limit on us. Is there no way to get at him, Nathan? Persuade him to withdraw and release the hostages? With time we can probably get him what he wants—the money restored."

"He'll never get another chance like this," Nathan said. "He hasn't got any reason to believe any promises. None of our people have any reason to believe promises."

"He can't win," Peter said. "Once he releases the hos-

145

tages the police will move in and wipe him out."

Nathan chuckled. "You don't think the prisoners are just going to walk out of the Warfield, do you? He'll get a free out from the police—if his terms have been met—and he'll take the hostages with him. They'll be released in different unnamed places, and Conway and his men will simply evaporate."

The chef came out of the kitchen, carrying his meat cleaver. He gestured toward the ceiling with it.

"Excuse me," Nathan said, and went back into the kitchen with the chef.

The voices at bar seemed to quiet. The men out there had been laughing and joking—but with their weapons ready. Now they seemed to be concentrating on the swinging doors to the kitchen.

The girl who appeared with Nathan was spectacular. She was tall, copper-colored, lithe. Her face, expertly made up, had high cheekbones, the mouth carefully painted, eyebrows over disturbingly brilliant eyes had been thinned. The long eyelashes, Peter thought at first were false, but as she came closer he saw that they weren't. She wore a very short miniskirt revealing magnificent legs, and a bright-colored blouse was cut in a very low V in front revealing the contours of luscious breasts. On a stage she would have drawn instant applause simply for her extraordinary beauty.

"Gloria Stewart—Peter Styles," Nathan said.

Peter felt the bright black eyes almost scorch him. "Murray died for you," she said.

"That's not quite the way it was, Gloria," Nathan said. He made some sort of signal to the bartender. "Murray and I asked Styles for help. He was doing for us, not us for him."

Nathan led her to the booth. The bartender brought her

a white crème-de-menthe with a brandy float on crushed ice. He had obviously known what she drank.

"I wouldn't have come, Nathan, if your boys hadn't made me," the girl said. "It's not safe for me here. It's not safe for me anywhere."

"No one's going to hurt you here, Gloria," Nathan said.

Peter slid over into the booth, facing her. Nathan sat beside him, preparing a fresh cigar.

"I don't know how much you know about what's going on, Gloria. Have you had a radio or a TV where you were?"

"Conway's played it too big for once," she said. "Murray always said he would. The money's gone, and it'll stay gone. It wasn't to talk about that you brought me here, Nathan."

"Tapes," Nathan said.

Peter could have sworn there was a brief flicker of fear in the girl's black eyes. "Tapes?" Her voice had an attractive throaty quality.

"There isn't much time, Gloria," Peter said. "The tapes are the one way we can hope to save those hostages Conway's holding. The tapes could persuade the Larkspur directors to replace the missing money."

"Why are you asking me? Why should I know about tapes? What tapes?"

"You want to play games, Gloria, I suppose we'll have to play games. A lot of people could die while we waltz around," Nathan said.

The girl raised a hand and touched her cheek with lacquered fingertips. "You remember a girl named Lucy Bolton?"

Nathan nodded.

Gloria looked at Peter. "Lucy did some talking the mob didn't like, Styles. She was a very a pretty girl. They

147

poured acid on her face."

"They cut out Murray's tongue," Nathan said quietly

"Oh, Jesus!" Gloria said, and covered her face with her hands. She was fighting for control. "That sweet guy." Her voice was unsteady. Finally she lowered her hands. " know there were tapes. But you knew Murray, Nathan."

"He loved you," Nathan said.

"Which is why he told me nothing!" Gloria said. "On night I found some tapes in his coat pocket. He was sleeping. After—well, he was sleeping. His coat was dirty, and thought I'd brush it and clean it up for him a little. I found two tapes in his pocket. He woke up and he saw them in my hands. He sounded angry, but I knew he was scared He grabbed the tapes out of my hand.

" 'Don't ever go through my clothes like that,' he said

"He saw I was shocked at the way he sounded. I mean Styles, we were close. Then he put his arms around me and I could feel he was trembling. 'I'm doing a job,' he said, ' didn't want you to know about it—anything about it. That way if anybody asked you, you wouldn't know.' I told him I still didn't know. 'So we keep it that way,' he said. 'You remember what happened to Lucy.' That was the same as telling me he was involved with Tony Larch, and I said so He admitted it, but he wouldn't tell me anything about it What I didn't know I couldn't tell anyone. That's what know about tapes. Or what I did know. When I heard what happened to Murray, and where it happened, I knew he'd provided you with the stuff you had in your article Peter. I—well, I knew more than I wanted to know. So went underground. I didn't think anyone could find me But if you found me, Nathan, Larch can find me."

"Murray had dozens of tapes, Gloria. Maybe a hundred tapes," Nathan said. "He had Larch's phone bugged. He was after him on drugs. But stuff about Larkspur came over the phone. Through me he passed it on to Styles. Now we need those tapes. Larch searched Styles's apartment, but they weren't there. He searched Murray's room. I don't think he found them there, because we think he's still looking. We need to find them before he does. Conway's hostages may die if we don't. Do you know where Murray kept them, where he hid them?"

"No!"

"Think, Gloria. Even if he didn't tell you you might be able to make an educated guess."

"If you had them you might be able to get Larch on a narcotics charge?"

"Might. And we might save those people Conway's holding."

"I don't give a damn for them, Nathan."

"Save them by getting the money back that was stolen from Larkspur," Nathan said. "A lot of people up here have been burned. Murray wanted to help them."

"But I don't know what you want to know!" Gloria said. "I don't know where he kept the tapes. I didn't press him about it because he didn't want me to know. Damn it, Nathan, I didn't want to know!" Once again her fingers touched her cheek.

"Crown was a secret kind of guy?" Peter asked.

"He was—in the time I knew him," Gloria said. "I—I didn't know him until after he was kicked off the police force. He talked about that when I first met him. We were living in a world of spies and counterspies, he said. He said cops couldn't do their job any more because they didn't know who they could trust. He said your own partner could be wired and reporting everything you said and did to someone else. He said he ought to know because he was an expert at wiring and bugging. He said more people were being listened to, and recorded, than you would believe—

by the cops, by the FBI, by the CIA, by big industry. He was paranoid about it, no kidding. He wouldn't even talk about anything serious in bed! His place or my place might be bugged. What I'm trying to say is, nothing ever slipped out of him by accident. He was always on guard."

"Which is why he came to your place, Styles, instead of waiting to get you on the phone. He didn't want to risk being overheard," Nathan said.

"Nathan tells me he lived in a single room up here in Harlem," Peter said.

"He never stayed in one place very long," Gloria said. "He was fighting the mob—on his own now, without any official help. He was really hiding all the time."

"But you knew where he was always?"

She shook her head. "Mostly he came to my place. Let me lay it on the line to you, Peter. We made love together, Murray and I. But we didn't live together. I never knew how to reach him. He came to me. I—God help me—I was always ready for him, always wanted him. Sometimes he was afraid even to spend an hour at my place. He'd have the idea that maybe he'd been followed. He'd arrange to meet me at a hotel somewhere when we were too hungry for each other to wait. He was always running—and I ran with him when he asked me to."

"So he wouldn't tell you anything because he loved you, and your knowing might have put you in danger," Peter said. "Was there no one else he trusted? No one from the old days on the force?"

"They kicked him out!"

"But the homicide man who's investigating his murder liked him, admired him. He told me that only yesterday."

"It's too bad Murray didn't know that. He felt he had no friends there. It hurt him."

"So he kept these tapes he made somewhere, Gloria."
150

"I can't help you."

"No friend who might be sitting on them for him?"

"If he did, he never mentioned anyone to me. Sweet Jesus, he was so careful of me. What I didn't know couldn't hurt me."

Nathan, his thoughts hidden behind the black glasses, studied the end of his cigar. "When Murray went to Styles's apartment yesterday we think he was trying to prevent a murder," he said. "He must have known the heat was on. He must have made some plan for those tapes—some way they'd get into the right hands if anything happened to him."

"I held him in my arms night before last," Gloria said, her voice shaken. "I knew, from the way he touched me, from the way his body felt against mine, that he was very uptight."

"He knew Styles's article was going to appear the next morning," Nathan said.

Time was moving on. Peter believed this girl. She didn't know what they needed to know. But Murray Crown, a careful professional, must have done something with those tapes. A man who was afraid to live in one room for more than a day or two wouldn't have kept them with him. He couldn't have carried them on him. A hundred tapes! He'd been risking his life to trap Larch. The tapes were part of the trap. They couldn't have been carelessly disposed of. But if neither Nathan nor Crown's girl had any idea where to look he was stymied.

"I don't know where your tapes are, Peter," Gloria said, "but—" She paused to take a little sip of her crème-de-menthe through a straw. "If there was any way I could help to square things for Murray—"

Nathan's black glasses stared at her steadily. "You forgotten Lucy Bolton?"

151

"I'm scared! I'm scared out of my life," Gloria said. "I don't want to get killed or hurt for nothing. I don't want Larch's men crawling all over me, or dropping acid on me, to make me tell something I don't know. But if there was a way I could help nail him for what he did to Murray—"

"Good girl," Nathan said.

Peter's eyes narrowed. "There just might be something," he said. "Let me make a phone call, Nathan."

"Be my guest," Nathan said. He tossed three or four dimes on the table.

It was time to call on Lieutenant Maxvil. Peter went into the phone booth and dialed the homicide man's home phone. It was answered promptly.

"I was told you wanted my help," Maxvil said. "I've been sitting here for two hours doing crossword puzzles, waiting to hear from you.

Peter told him where he was and what had happened to him getting here.

"You want a police escort to bring you out?"

"Crown's girl, Gloria Stewart, is here with us," Peter said. "Larch's people think I came up here for the tapes. If they saw me with Gloria they might think she was taking me to them. I don't think they'd grab us; I think they'd follow us."

"To where?" Maxvil said.

"Somewhere you'll be waiting. You name it," Peter said. "At the least you could put them out of circulation for a while. At best they might reveal something useful."

"It might work," Maxvil said. "Let me make it airtight. In twenty minutes I'll have cops watching up there. You leave. Larch follows. We follow Larch. That's just in case, Peter—in case Larch thinks it would be more efficient to grab you and the girl and try his special methods to force you into talking. As I remember, the Stewart girl is somehink of a dish. Does she want to risk being carved up?"

"If it will help."

"Do you want her to risk it?" Maxvil asked.

"Greg, time is running out on us. Elaine Summers and seventy-three other people may not make it alive unless I can bring some kind of solid pressure to bear on the Larkspur Board."

"What good is Larch under arrest going to do you?"

"He might talk."

"No chance."

"Somebody may think he might talk," Peter said. "If anybody makes a tiny false move we may get a lead. Right now, without Crown's tapes, we've got nothing.

"It's a very slim chance for the risk involved," Maxvil said.

"A slim chance is better than no chance at all."

Maxvil appeared to make up his mind. "Okay, I'll buy it," he said. "Give me the number you're calling from. I'll call you back to let you know our men are ready to cover you on the street. Then you and the girl start out."

"Start out to where, Greg?"

Maxvil chuckled. "Why not right here to my place? My name isn't on the doorbell, you know. 'John Smith' lives in the first-floor apartment at the rear."

CHAPTER 4

IT WAS A very slim chance. The possible results came a long way from outweighing the possible risks. Nathan thought the scheme would produce exactly nothing. He agreed with Maxvil that Larch, if in fact he was part of the picture, would never do any talking. Larch's men had the memory of what had happened to Crown to convince them that anything was better than talking.

But there might be something! Some small slip. Some small revelation that would put them on the track. Gloria was frightened but willing.

Nathan was prepared to produce a taxi, driven by a friend, to pick them up outside the bar and take them downtown. It took Maxvil nearly half an hour to make his return call. Peter, glancing at his watch, saw that it was just after four. There would be the beginnings of daylight before too very long.

"My men are in place up there," Maxvil said. "It isn't too late to change your mind, Peter."

"What else to try?" Peter asked.

"You would expect to be followed," Maxvil said. "Tell your driver not to act as if he was trying to shake a tail—

eeping coming right on down Fifth Avenue—not fast—
ot slow."

It was time to go.

Nathan's taxi was waiting. Aside from a couple of light-
ss parked cars down the block the street seemed to be
eserted. There was that ominous kind of silence Peter had
een aware of when he first arrived uptown. He had been
p here at night before. There was always the sound of
usic behind some lighted windows, the street corner
oungers, the all-night coffee shops. There was nothing but
reet lights outside Nathan's place. The whole area was
ill, dark, inactive; yet Peter had the sensation that hun-
reds of very wide-awake people were watching them
rom hundreds of vantage points. Watching and waiting
or violence to break loose.

The driver of the green and white taxi already had his
astructions from Nathan. Peter and Gloria got in. They sat
ery close together, and Peter could feel her lacquered fin-
ernails biting into the skin of his wrist.

The taxi started up. Instantly one of the parked cars
noved, without lights, and pulled in a couple of car lengths
ehind them. If that was Larch's car, where in hell were
Maxvil's men? Peter, staring into the rearview mirror,
ouldn't tell if the second parked car had also moved. If
: had it was also traveling without lights.

Peter could feel Gloria's body pressed against him, trem-
ling.

"You read about it in the papers," she said, "but you
vouldn't be able to guess what it's like, living in our world
p here."

"I may know more than most people," Peter said. "My
vife—"

"Nathan told me about her. I've heard people up here
aention her. She was well liked." Gloria's hand tightened

on his arm. "This has been a bad time for people: Murray taken from me, your wife taken from you, Elaine's husband taken from her. Did Nathan tell you I worked in a show with Elaine?"

"No."

"Real wild woman," Gloria said.

"How do you mean?"

"I mean talented, I mean exciting, I mean great to work with and for. Wild—like she's an original. She is a star, but she treats everyone in the company like a next-door neighbor. You know something, Styles? She's not scared for herself right now, but she's dying for those other people Conway's got locked up. That's the way she is."

Peter looked up at the rearview mirror. The trailing car had switched on its parking lights. They were in that no man's land between 110th and 125th Streets Peter had noticed on the way up. Dead—no people—no lights. If Larch meant to stop them, this was the place to do it, but the following car kept its distance.

"When were you with Elaine?" Peter asked. Gloria seemed to relax a little when she was talking.

"Season before last," Gloria said. "Show called *Honey Pot*. Did you see it?"

"No. I wish I had. I'd like to have seen you on stage. You must light up the sky a little yourself."

"I sing and dance, I look pretty good, I guess. But Elaine's not just a musical comedy chick. She's a performer, an actress, a star."

"Did you know her husband?"

"He was courting her then. They married right after the show closed."

"Did that surprise you?"

The taxi had reached 110th Street. The park was straight ahead of them. The driver cut east and then headed down
156

ifth Avenue. Peter saw a red glow beginning to show
ehind the buildings in Queens. It would soon be light.
Gloria leaned back in the seat, and her grip on Peter's arm
oosened.

"I didn't really think Larch would let us come this far,"
he said. Her eyelids lowered, and the long lashes caressed
er cheeks. "Yes, I was surprised Elaine married Walter
Girard. Oh, he was a nice enough man, courteous, thought-
ul. He was really off his head about her. But—but Elaine
ould have chosen anyone in the world she wanted. And
ou should have seen the boys who were after her, Peter.
Movie stars, big-time sports stars, and—well, some of the
est-looking young studs you ever laid eyes on. I'd have
nvied her if it hadn't been for Murray. I figured her for a
irl who had a pretty big appetite for sex—an appetite a
nan in his late fifties might find it pretty hard to satisfy.
To tell you the truth, I was surprised she married anyone.
he could play the field; she could pick and choose. There
re some women—not many—who have so much vitality,
o much juice, that no one man can keep up with them. A
voman like that doesn't usually marry except for money."

"Elaine doesn't need money from what I hear," Peter
aid.

"Which is why I was surprised when she married Mr.
Girard," Gloria said.

Peter turned his head toward her lovely, coppery face.
"Did you think she was playing around?"

Gloria shrugged. "One thing about Elaine," she said.
"Her public life was very public, and her private life was
ery private."

They were cruising past the Public Library. The city
treets were still relatively deserted, even downtown. Win-
lows of the great department stores were dimly lit, more
or protection than display. They were stopping now for

157

the changing traffic lights. A police car crossed in front of them heading east. Peter felt Gloria's fingers tighten on his wrist again.

"How much farther?" she asked.

"Not far. The apartment's on East Thirty-sixth Street. We should be making the next left turn."

"An apartment house?"

"Remodeled brownstone," Peter said.

"No doorman or anything?"

"No."

"Peter, I haven't seen anything that looks like cops following us—only that one car."

"I know."

"You suppose they missed us?"

"We just keep going till we get to Maxvil's," Peter said. He'd been asking himself the same question. There'd been no sign at any part of the trip downtown of a second car following.

The cab turned east on Thirty-sixth Street and Peter felt his muscles growing tense. They crossed Madison, and then Park, and the driver edged over toward the south side of the street. The trailing car was no more than twenty yards behind them as the taxi stopped. The driver turned in his seat.

"The ride's on Nathan," he said. "They stuck pretty close. Nathan said not to try to shake them. When you get out I'm pulling away. Looks like there's four of them in the car."

"Thanks," Peter said. The brownstone was dark except for a dim light in the first-floor foyer, half a dozen steps up from the sidewalk. The basement apartment, Peter knew, was occupied by an artist. He looked at Gloria. "Take hold of my arm when we get out and we go straight up the steps into that foyer. Don't stop to look back. Remember
158

hat happened to Lot's wife."

He stepped out onto the pavement and Gloria came after
m. One quick glance showed him that men were getting
t of the following car. They went quickly up the steps
d into the foyer. Peter searched, in the semidarkness, for
e name John Smith on the brass mailboxes with the door-
ll buttons over them, found it, and pressed hard on the
tton.

Almost instantly there was the clicking sound of the lock
eing released from the inside. He leaned against the door
push it open—and felt Gloria's hand being wrenched
vay from his wrist. She screamed, and was instantly silent.
omeone pushed him hard and he stumbled through the
oor into the inner hallway. As he regained his balance and
rned he found himself faced by a smiling dark-haired
an holding a gun that was aimed straight at Peter's chest.

"Keep right on moving, Styles," the man said.

A second man had moved to the foot of the stairs and
as looking up, obviously concerned that Gloria's scream
ight have alarmed someone. Two other men had Gloria,
e by each arm, holding her just inside the street door.

"We'll keep the lady here," the smiling man said, "just
case you got any tricks up your sleeve."

"Who the hell are you?" Peter asked.

"My, my, I'm disappointed," the smiling man said. "Big
ot like you, making headlines, doesn't know who I am.
et's not play games with each other, pal. I want those
pes of Crown's worse than you do. What else would you
e doing running around town with a black girl unless she
as taking you to where they were?"

"You're Larch!" Peter said.

"Antonio Larchesi in the priest's book," Larch said.
Where do we go? Or do I have my boys get the girl to
ll us?"

159

"Peter!" Gloria cried out.

He had fallen for it, Peter thought. But in the next minute or two it might not have been worth it. He hoped to God Maxvil had anticipated this possibility.

"Apartment at the end of the hall," he said. "John Smith."

"Somebody should have had more imagination than that," Larch said. "Let's get a bright clear picture of things, Styles. The girl stays out here with my kids. Let's hope her yelling hasn't got anyone stirring upstairs. We might have to cut her up a little if that happens. And if you pull anything we'll cut her up good. You wouldn't like the looks of her if that happens."

Peter tried the only thing he could think of. "I need her to vouch for me," he said. "Smith doesn't know me."

"He doesn't have to know you," Larch said, still with that frozen smile on his dark face. "All he has to do is open the door. Once we get in there he'll give us the tapes."

"Peter!" This time it was a hoarse whisper from Gloria.

"Keep it cool, baby, if you want anyone to look at that nice black body of yours again. Now move, Styles." Larch pushed the muzzle of his gun forward. "We can go in without you, you know, if you make it tough."

Peter turned and moved slowly down the dark hallway to the door at the end. There was a little brass bracket with the name John Smith inserted in it on a card.

"Ring the bell," Larch said.

Peter's finger felt numb as he touched the button. When the door opened all hell was likely to break loose and he was in the middle.

The door opened a few inches. There was a guard chain on it. A completely unfamiliar voice said: "Who it it?"

Larch's gun pressed hard into Peter's back.

160

"Peter Styles," Peter said. "Gloria says—"

"Just a minute," the strange voice said. The door closed and they could hear the chain being unhooked. Then the door opened and a mild-looking little man Peter had never seen before faced them. Larch gave Peter a violent shove past the little man and he and his extra man, now also showing a gun, burst into the apartment behind him. Larch's man closed the apartment door. The strange little man had been hurled back against a sofa. His eyes were wide with what appeared to be surprise.

Peter looked around, thinking he must have made some ghastly mistake. It was Maxvil's apartment. He remembered the pictures on the wall, the big overstuffed armchair by the fireplace.

"You're John Smith?" Larch asked the little man.

"Sure," the little man said. "What are you doing here? What do you mean by breaking into my apartment?"

"The tapes, man," Larch said.

"What do you mean, tapes? What tapes?" The little man stood leaning against the couch, breathing hard. "I don't know anything about any tapes."

"The tapes Murray Crown left with you," Larch said. He was still smiling, but it looked pasted on. His voice was harsh.

"I don't know any Crown," the little man said. "Nobody left any tapes with me."

"You're a lying sonofabitch, Mr. Smith," Larch said. He turned to his man. "Eddie, see if you can revive Mr. Smith's memory a little."

Eddie was a big, muscular man with a broken-nose face. He turned his gun around in his hand so that it became a club and moved toward the little man.

"You ever been pistol-whipped, Mr. Smith?" Larch

161

asked. "I don't recommend it for fun and games, but w
don't have time to persuade you some other way. You wa
to tell us where the tapes are?"

The little man was staring at Eddie. He didn't answer.

"Okay, Eddie, work him over," Larch said.

What happened then was so unbelievable that Peter a
most missed a key moment. Eddie swung his gun at th
little man's head, but it didn't make contact. Somehow th
little man blocked it, moved with unexpected speed to on
side, and Eddie was suddenly hurtling over the little man
shoulder, over the couch, and head on into the far wall. Th
little man was after him like a small tiger.

Larch had turned away from Peter, not believing wha
he saw. He raised his gun to fire at the little man, an
Peter knocked it out of his hand and swung a backhande
blow to Larch's jaw. Larch went down, scrambling for th
gun.

"I wouldn't pick that up if I were you, buster."

Peter spun around. Maxvil was standing in the door t
the bedroom, pointing a police special at Larch's head
There was a man standing behind the Lieutenant, and tw
other men came out of the kitchen.

"Nice work, Peter," Maxvil said. "Saved me from havin
to plug him. This way he'll talk better." He turned towar
the little man. "I wouldn't have believed it, Arty," he sai
"You ought to get a black belt for that one. How is he?"

"Out cold," the little man said, grinning. "Hit his hea
real good." There was nothing mild or frightened abou
him now.

"You should meet Sergeant Arthur Trotter, Peter," Ma
vil said. "Best karate man on the force. Truth is he alread
has a black belt."

The other men were handcuffing Larch and his uncor
scious friend.

"Greg, the girl is out there in the hall," Peter said. "Two of Larch's men have got her out there."

"Correction," Maxvil said. " 'Had' her out there."

He walked over to the front door and opened it. Gloria came running into the room followed by a plain-clothesman. Peter found her in his arms, laughing and crying.

"Sorry to keep you in suspense," Maxvil said. "We had a bug on the taxi so we followed you downtown, east of you all the way." He walked over to the desk and opened a drawer. He brought out a small tape machine and turned it off. "There was a tape here, Larch, but not the one you were looking for. This one's got enough on it to drive your smart lawyers crazy." He took a step forward and gave the handcuffed Larch a violent shove that sent him sprawling back on the couch. "Now, you miserable bastard, let's get down to business."

Larch wasn't smiling any more.

Maxvil was rewinding the tape on his little machine. "You are going to wish to God, Larch, that you never heard the word 'tape,' " he said, anger gone from his voice. He tapped the little recorder. "You've tied yourself into Crown, you're guilty of breaking and entering, assaulting a police officer, threats of violence against Styles and Miss Stewart. When the tapes you're looking for do turn up—and I suspect they will because Crown was far too clever to leave them where they couldn't be found if anything happened to him—you will undoubtedly find yourself facing the next hundred years in jail on narcotics charges, even if I don't get you for Crown's murder." Maxvil's voice hardened. "Let me see, I am required to inform you of your rights. Sergeant Trotter, will you read our friend the rigmarole about a suspect's rights."

Maxvil touched Peter's arm and shepherded him and Gloria to the far corner of the room. The little karate expert began to read something to Larch out of a small note book. He sounded like a priest reading a long meaningles ritual.

"Sorry to give you such a bad time, Miss Stewart," Max vil said.

She was still trembling, clinging to Peter. "I was neve so scared in my whole life," she said. "One of them ha a knife he kept waving under my nose. And then your me seemed to appear out of nowhere!"

"For once in my life I guessed exactly right on what the would do," Maxvil said. "Larch is tough, but not ver subtle." He looked at Peter. "I've got him cold for the tim being as far as I'm concerned, Peter. What we can get ou of him to help you is something else again. You got ideas?

"Is his lawyer Callahan?" Peter said. "Who had acces to his office phone in Harlem who is also connected wit Larkspur? Who is 'Tom'?"

"That one tape you have doesn't give us much in the wa of voice quality," Maxvil said. "The man talking to 'Tom could have been Larch himself. Larkspur isn't the kind o racket I'd expect Larch to go in for—too many people no under Syndicate disciplines involved; too many people wh might crack under pressure and talk. But there's so damne much money involved he could have gotten greedy." H drew a deep breath. "Well, we can try." He turned bac to the couch. "You dotted all the i's and crossed all the t's Trotter?"

"I read it all to him," the little karate expert said.

"So do you want me to send for Callahan?" Maxvil aske Larch.

Larch had turned stone-faced. "Who is Callahan?" h asked.

"Isn't Andrew Callahan your lawyer?"

"Never heard of him," Larch said. "My lawyer i
164

Bernard Gottlieb, and I want to send for him before I do any talking."

"Ah yes, little Bernie Gottlieb," Maxvil said. "We know him well in the department. I'm afraid this time Bernie is going to wind up with egg on his face. But send for him. Use the telephone—unless you'd prefer to do this whole thing downtown at headquarters. I can imagine that at this moment you're wishing that Alexander Graham Bell had never invented the telephone, but help yourself."

"What's happened to my men who were outside?" Larch asked.

"Maybe I should consult my lawyer before answering that," Maxvil said, "but what the hell, why shouldn't I tell you? They're on their way to adjoining jail cells, charged with attempted kidnapping, threatening Miss Stewart with a knife, breaking and entering, and a few other odds and ends, like resisting arrest."

"I want to call Gottlieb."

"Fine." Maxvil sounded smooth as oil. "You know his number? I'll dial it for you. Complicated to dial with those irons on you."

Larch gave him a number and Maxvil dialed. After a moment someone answered. "Gottlieb?" Maxvil asked. "Sorry to call you so late—or is it so early? Lieutenant Maxvil of Homicide. I've got a client of yours in custody— Tony Larch. He needs you real badly, Bernie. He's at 136½ East 36th Street, first-floor apartment at the rear. Name of John Smith. Don't bother waking up a judge, Bernie. This time no writs or habeas corpuses are going to work. I've got this butcher cold." He put down the phone. "Bernie will toddle over," he said. "Now, Antonio Larchesi, or Anthony Larch, or Tony—you are way the hell and gone up the creek. When Crown's tapes turn up you have had it. You know that, or you wouldn't have run the risks you've run tonight. Personal risks, which is unlike you. I have enough on you to hold you till Christmas, if it takes that long to find those tapes. But you might be able to help yourself a little."

"You're offering me a deal?" Larch asked, looking surprised.

"No deal, Tony. But a judge might take into consideration a willingness to cooperate when it comes to passing sentence. For example, who in the Larkspur setup had access to your Harlem telephone? Because we do have one tape, Tony, that started Styles on the Larkspur case."

You could almost see the wheels turning inside Larch's skull, Peter thought. "I don't know anything about Larkspur," he said finally.

"Yet you went looking for tapes in Styles's apartment," Maxvil said.

"I've never been in Styles's apartment in my life."

"Possibly. Was it your knife-waving friend out in the hall who murdered Crown and cut out his tongue?"

Larch moistened dry lips. "You're dreaming," he said.

"Did you contract with someone named Tom to knock off Walter Girard?" Maxvil waited. "Who is Tom?"

Larch actually laughed. "You really are dreaming up a storm, Maxvil," he said. "There's no way I can cooperate when I don't know what you're talking about."

"Were those your men who posed as cops and fired on Conway's hostages from the roof of the Warfield?" Peter asked.

There was a quick shift of attention from Larch, but he didn't answer.

"How did you know I was leaving the Selwyn and have your men waiting in a car to follow me?"

Larch looked down at the handcuffs on his wrists. "I can cooperate just a little bit on that one, Styles," he said. "In my line of work you've got ears all over the place. When

I—when I read in the paper that Murray Crown had been hit at your place, I put one and one together and made two. He was a bugging expert. I had no doubt he was after me. Life work for a stupid do-gooder like Crown. I checked out my Harlem business phone and found it bugged. I guessed that Crown had turned over tapes to you, or told you where they were. So"—he shrugged—"I arranged to stay with you till you took me to them. My men screwed things up by shooting at you up in Harlem. If they'd let you alone, you'd probably have taken me to the tapes instead of here."

Peter turned away. They had Larch set up for a long stay in prison, but they didn't have answers. He had used up three hours of time and he still had nothing to go on.

The Selwyn Hotel looked like the morning after. The lobby was still crowded with people, some of whom were asleep in the lobby chairs. The place was littered with candy wrappers and empty cigarette packs. In the office behind the reception desk Captain McGraw sat, red-eyed and needing a shave.

"Any luck?" he asked, when Peter came in.

"Not that will do us much good in the time we have," Peter said. "Larch is out of circulation, but he isn't going to be any use to us in time. What about here?"

"Quiet." A nerve twitched in McGraw's cheek. "Like I thought, those two cops who came out on the roof were not cops. We found the uniforms, the guns, the vests, the helmets all in a deserted apartment in the building next door. Whoever they were they just evaporated. Working for someone we goddamn well need to find."

"Could be Larch," Peter said, "but it isn't something we can prove in a hurry. What's happened to the Larkspur Board?"

"They broke up a little while ago," McGraw said. "Still

167

arguing about who's responsible for what. They're supposed to meet back here at nine o'clock."

"Frank Devery's bringing the one tape we have," Peter said. "I'm going to play it for the Board. The voice quality is bad, but someone honest—if there is someone honest—might hear something."

McGraw looked beaten. "You can get some coffee and breakfast in the bar here if you want it. I can't believe the Larkspur people won't come through with something at the last minute. If they don't, God help us."

"It's a hell of a lot of money to raise in a short time, no matter how honest they are."

Peter realized that he was very hungry. He went out through the lobby to the bar. The first person he saw, sitting at a corner table, was Andrew Callahan. The lawyer was drinking something that looked like a Bloody Mary. He saw Peter and gestured to him to join him.

"They say you went looking for tapes," he said. "Any luck?"

"No."

"The whole damned business goes round and round in my head and doesn't come out anywhere," Callahan said. "Sit down. Talking to someone might help." Then he seemed to remember. "Any news about your wife?"

"Nothing."

A waiter stopped by the table and Peter ordered scrambled eggs and bacon and a pot of coffee. He realized he must look as done-in as most of the people around the hotel. Callahan pointed to his glass and suggested to the waiter that he make the new drink a double.

"I have a question," Peter said. "You're a man who's used to dealing with the very rich. Can that Board of Directors get up twenty million dollars in the course of a business day?"

168

Callahan laughed. "Take them a long time, like fifteen minutes. I'm not talking about in unmarked one-dollar bills, you understand. There are only two or three poor men on that Board, Styles, and you and I wouldn't think of them as poor. Bracket, the treasurer, is just a paid figure man—paid about fifty grand a year. The Cantwell Construction Company must provide Ted McCauley with an income of about a hundred grand a year. His mother's family owned it. Ted started out as a hod carrier—bricklayer. Got to be president. Horatio Alger stuff. Boswell, the Deputy Mayor, doesn't have a dime of his own, but his family is loaded. The rest of them together have a hell of a lot better credit than the United States Treasury. No problem about raising the money if they decide to."

"Surely they must, then. So what are we sweating about?"

Callahan shook his head. It seemed to take an effort. "What a man will do when his money is involved is never a very certain thing. I've spent the last twenty-four hours trying to understand why my best and oldest friend, a rich man, chose to steal a fortune he didn't need."

"There's no question about that? Girard wasn't in some secret trouble?"

"I told you yesterday morning; no trouble at all. That's the one thing in all this I know to be a fact. He is loaded. Elaine is loaded. Yet he acted so strangely when your story appeared." Callahan finished his drink and looked longingly toward the waiter at the bar.

"Tell me again," Peter said.

"*Newsview* came out on the stands that morning with your story in it," Callahan said. "My secretary brought it in to me. She was, to coin a cliché, white as a sheet. I read it, called Walter at his office. He sounded faraway, like a man in a trance. He said he hadn't seen the magazine. I gave

169

him the essential facts—suspicion that money was missing, a tape that allegedly accused him of setting up Swiss bank accounts for the money, all the rest of it. He acted as if I'd just told him someone had accused him of voting for George McGovern last year."

"Not shocked?"

"Not really listening," Callahan said. "I wanted to go straight over to his office to talk—to help. He refused. Said he was tied up. Said there was nothing to it, I shouldn't worry. Well, I worried. I called Ted McCauley, Chairman of the Board. He reacted. Jesus, how he reacted. He called me back in a while. He was really worried. He said Walter was acting like a sleepwalker; wouldn't talk. Said he had some private matters to attend to and to hell with the *Newsview* story."

"He must have taken it seriously later," Peter said. "According to Elaine he was very much concerned when he came to see her after the matinee. 'I'm going to have it out with some of the pricks who must have done this to me.' No truth in it."

"At four o'clock in the afternoon he still wouldn't see me," Callahan said. "He wouldn't even talk to me on the phone. I didn't know till it was all over that he'd gone to see Elaine. I guess when a man is thinking of blowing out his brains he's pretty unpredictable."

"You still buy suicide?" Peter asked. He wondered if this whole harangue was designed to get him off the murder theory again.

"Elaine wants to believe in him," Callahan said. "That's typical of her—loyal person. But if you'd talked to him that day you'd know he was at the breaking point. I asked myself, when I heard what had happened, why does a man commit suicide? He could have a terminal illness he

170

couldn't face. Walter'd had a checkup about six weeks ago. Clean bill. He could be facing a financial disaster. Walter's affairs are in great shape. I know; I handle them. He could have been betrayed by someone he loved. Well, you know Elaine and how she felt about him. He could be about to be exposed as a degenerate or a criminal. That had to be it —a criminal. Why, God only knows."

"Young Gary Lehman sounded as sure about Girard as you do," Peter said. "A man of enormous integrity. Like you, he was completely puzzled."

Callahan lifted his heavy eyelids to give the waiter a grateful look as he delivered the fresh Bloody Mary and Peter's eggs.

"You went to see Gary, then?" Callahan asked.

"Elaine asked me to. He backed up her statements about Girard's honesty."

"And about her fidelity to Walter? I guess that's why she wanted you to see him." Callahan swallowed. "There's been talk."

"About Elaine and Gary?"

"Gary has made out with most of the wives of most of his friends—and most of the daughters of his older friends," Callahan said. "He is the stud to end all studs. The fact that he didn't have any luck with Elaine is proof enough of her devotion to Walter."

At that moment Peter saw Frank Devery standing in the doorway to the bar and signaled to him. Devery looked fresh and rested. Peter knew he had been up all night.

"You brought the tape?" he asked, after introducing Devery to Callahan.

Devery patted his pocket. "When does the Board meet again?"

"Nine o'clock."

171

"Time for you to freshen up so you don't look like the ghost of Hamlet's father," Devery said. "It's on the news ticker that you nailed Larch."

Peter described his trip to Harlem and back.

"It's really two stories," Devery said, "which isn't fair to the working press. If we come up with those missing tapes, the drug business is going to blow sky-high. You can bet that's why Larch is so eager for them. You can't run his kind of racket without some people in high places smoothing the way for him; cops, city officials. It will be a big one when it breaks. But right now we've got to get those poor jerks away from Conway. When you play this tape for the Board I want to be there. I want them to know the kind of publicity they're going to get if they hesitate too long."

The eggs tasted like sawdust. Somewhere in the back of his mind Peter sensed an idea beginning to percolate, something that hadn't occurred to him before, but he couldn't put his finger on it. The coffee was bitter.

The Larkspur directors assembled in that private dining room a little after nine o'clock. As a group they looked harried and worn. Devery was present, and Captain McGraw and Commissioner Ryan. Marshall was missing. At the far end of the room Gary Lehman gestured a hello to Peter. It would be his job, as P.R. man for Larkspur, to prepare any kind of public statement that was to come from the Board.

Peter and Devery were at the head of the table next to McCauley.

"The Mayor is back in town," McCauley told them. "He's on a hot line to the Governor and maybe to the White House."

"Why do you need help?" Devery asked. "The answer to

your problem is right here in this room. You can raise the money right here if you want."

"It's not easy," McCauley said. "If we had more time. If the really big shots would guarantee it— What's this tape you want to play for us?"

"Very short. But it started it all," Devery said.

"We hope some of you may recognize voices," Peter said. "The tape is pretty scratchy, but there's a chance."

"Girard is the man who did us in," McCauley said.

"Maybe," Peter said. "But this tape will indicate that he had friends. Can we run it for them now?"

McCauley pounded on the table with a heavy glass ashtray to bring the meeting to order. Devery was setting up the little tape machine. Peter, his legs feeling weak under him, sat down in a chair next to McCauley. Lying in front of him on the table was a typed list of the Board members. "Theodore Osborn McCauley, Chairman; Vincent Boswell—" and on and on. You might have called it a list of Wall Street royalty. Ralph Cushing, the white-haired president of Seaways Oil, sat a few chairs away, chin sunk down on his chest, eyes closed. He looked like a man who had spent his life waiting for the inconsequential preliminaries to be done with, waiting for what was really important to begin.

"I have here," Devery told the trustees, "a very brief tape recording. The telephone of a notorious Syndicate gangster was tapped. Tony Larch, czar of the drug business in Harlem. His phone was illegally tapped, by the way. The man who did it was an ex-cop—an ex-black-cop—named Crown. You probably read about his murder in the newspaper, or heard about it on TV or radio. He taped hours of phone conversations that came over Larch's line. Some of them were legitimate insurance business, Larch's cover. Some had to do with the drug racket, in which

173

Crown was interested. But there was just one that had to do with something else that concerned Crown—Larkspur. I'm going to play it for you, and then I'm going to play it again. Our hope is that some of you may recognize voices. Please listen."

The tape began to wind. And then the voices came, scratchy and distorted.

"*Tom? I thought you should know that Girard has arranged for two numbered Swiss bank accounts.*"

"*Great.*"

"*The money will have been transferred in a few days. It will certainly be a few months before anybody begins to smell a rat.*"

"*And then?*"

"*Then we proceed as planned.*"

The tape continued to turn but there was no more sound. Devery switched it off.

"That conversation took place about three weeks ago," he said. "The tape, just as you hear it, was turned over to Styles. He researched it and we printed his story. Anyone recognize a voice?"

There was a dead silence around the table.

"Anyone care to identify someone called Tom?"

The directors looked at each other. "I know a dozen 'Toms'" Ralph Cushing said impatiently. "I don't happen to recall anyone on this Board named Tom. You have the list up there, McCauley. Do we have a Tom?"

Peter had been doodling on the list, listening to the tape he'd heard half a hundred times. McCauley took the list and glanced down it. "I know already, Ralph, that there is no Tom, or Thomas, or Thompson on this list." He folded up the list and put it in his inside jacket pocket.

"Listen once more," Devery said. "I know the quality is bad. Listen for a familiar inflection, a familiar way of

174

lking."

The tape scratched out its record once more. When it
as finished there was a kind of mass headshaking, a nega-
ve muttering.

"Well, we tried, gentlemen," Devery said. His face had
hard, grim look to it. "Now let me tell you something.
ou can raise the money right in his room to free those
ostages. I recommend that you raise it unless you want to
e publicized, all over the world, as murderers."

There was an instant clamor of protest. Old Ralph
ushing was suddenly on his feet, pounding on the table.
Ie got attention.

"Let's cut out all this time-wasting indignation," he said.
We all know we've got to get up the money." He turned
 Peter. "Can you get back inside that theater again to
lk to Conway?"

"I think so," Peter said. "I can also talk to him on the
hone."

"The phone isn't good enough," Cushing said. "He
vants assurances from us. We want assurances from him.
Ve have to know for certain that those hostages are alive
nd unharmed. How do we convince Conway that the
noney is back in the fund? How will the hostages be
eleased? That's all too complicated for a phone call, and
ou've got to see those hostages and report back to us.
Vill you go in?"

"Of course," Peter said.

"Good. Call Conway and tell him you're coming. Give
s fifteen minutes to work out the money plan. Then you
o in."

Peter felt the blood pounding at his temples. He stood
p, feeling unsteady. In the last moments, while the direc-
ors had wrangled, he had experienced something not unlike
going to a play. He had been sitting in front of a dropped

175

curtain, not having any idea what lay behind it. He ha
been doodling on McCauley's list of directors, listenin
to the familiar tape, listening to the back-and-forth, an
the curtain had gone up on that theater in his mind and h
had seen what it must be all about. It was like watchin
half a dozen pieces of a multipiece puzzle fit neatly to
gether, leaving the rest relatively simple. He needed th
answers to two or three questions, not too hard to com
by, and it would all be there. He looked down at the fa
end of the room, hunting for Gary Lehman, but the publi
relations man had slipped away. He was suddenly awar
that Ralph Cushing was tugging at his arm.

"What's the matter with you, Styles? You asleep?"

"Sorry," Peter said vaguely.

The old man's pale eyes were sharp and shrewd. "You
come up with something? You look like a man with
answers."

"Maybe."

Cushing's fingers bit hard into Peter's arm. "First thing
first," he said. "There are seventy-odd people across th
street whose lives depend on our handling this correctly
Call Conway and tell him you'll be coming over in half a
hour. Check back with me in twenty minutes. You car
wait that long to be a hero, can't you?"

"You're right, of course," Peter said, still faraway.

Cushing literally shook Peter. "I saw you looking at tha
list of directors. You came up with the answer, didn't you.
Well, *so did I!* But those people across the way come first.'

Peter turned to look at the old man. "You saw it?"

"Yes, my young friend, I saw it," Cushing said. "Bu
first we deal with Conway. After that we can handle ou
mutual friend. Move!"

Peter walked slowly out of the crowded room and acros
the lobby to McGraw's office. It was deserted. He picke

p the phone like a man in a dream and dialed the number the Warfield that would reach Conway.

"Time's running out," Conway said, when he came to the hone.

"The deal is ready to be made except for details. I have come across to talk to you in, say half an hour, more or less."

"Call me when you're starting," Conway said.

"I'll be asking you what will satisfy you that they're on he level. And I'll insist on knowing how you propose to elease the hostages and I'll want to see them all to be sure ney're all right."

"One girl is critical; the one who was shot in the chest. he doctor seems to be doing what he can. I'll have nswers for you."

Peter put down the phone. He felt lightheaded. He went ut of the office and started across the lobby toward the nen's room. He had the childish notion that cold water on is face and wrists would bring him down to earth. He topped halfway, seeing Gary Lehman at one of the house hones.

Lehman saw Peter. He finished his phone call and came uickly over. "All set with Conway?" he asked. A strange allor showed through his perpetual sun tan.

"It's arranged," Peter said.

"You'll be seeing Elaine when you go over?"

"I'll be seeing everybody," Peter said in a flat voice.

"Tell her—tell her I'll be waiting for her," Gary said.

"This would have been an easier ball game to play if ou weren't a goddamn liar," Peter said.

Gary moistened his lips. "It—I couldn't play it any other vay, Peter."

"I wouldn't have thought nobility was your style," Peter aid.

177

"Tell Elaine you guessed it; that I didn't tell you," Gary said. He shook his head. "She loved him, in spite of everything. He just didn't have what it took to—to take care of her physical needs. What good can it do for everyone to know that he was cuckolded?"

"He killed himself because he found out that you were in the hay with his wife," Peter said. "He wasn't concerned with Larkspur, or my article, or who the thieves were. He never told Elaine that he was going to find out who'd done him in, right? You'd brought his world crashing down around him. He didn't give a damn about anything else. That's why he wouldn't talk to Callahan or McCauley or anyone else."

"I never felt sorry for the 'other man' before," Gary said. "He was a decent guy. I was sorry we hurt him so badly."

"We've spent a lot of energy hunting for a killer when you two were it," Peter said. "You killed him just as surely as if you'd pulled the trigger."

"An infidelity. It hurts, but who could dream he'd kill himself? One thing you need to know in all this mess," Gary said. "Girard did open at least one Swiss bank account. It was for Elaine. Tax reasons."

"Or were you planning to run out on him anyway?" Peter asked.

"It could have happened," Gary said. "It was getting so I couldn't bear to share her with anyone. God help me, for the first time in my life I'm in love with someone!"

"What did Girard burn in that metal wastebasket?"

Gary shook his head. "I've no idea, Peter. Some part of his life he didn't want to leave behind him."

"You make me feel just a little bit sick," Peter said. He pushed past Gary and went on into the men's room.

There were four washbasins in the room. Peter took of

is jacket and tie and hung them on a hook. He went to one of the basins and turned on the cold water. He bent down, cupping his hands, and doused his face with water. There was a mildly pleasurable shock to it. He reached out for a towel, and heard the door open behind him. He turned, blotting at his eyes. McCauley and the two other men had come in. One of the men stood with his back to the door, leaning against it. The second man stood beside McCauley.

McCauley reached in his pocket and took out a folded sheet of paper. It was the list of Larkspur directors.

"Your scribbling on this kind of gave you away, Styles," McCauley said. "Theodore Osborn McCauley, Chairman. And under it you wrote my initials—T.O.M. Came over you all of a sudden, didn't it?"

Peter stood where he was, drying his hands on the towel. So every game comes to an end, McCauley," he said.

"True, but unfortunately for you, the game that's got to come to an end is yours, Styles."

"Hard to give up with twenty million bucks waiting for you somewhere," Peter said.

"Impossible to give up," McCauley said. "My friends here have a piece of it coming, and one or two others."

"Like Bracket, your treasurer, who had to overlook missing checks?"

McCauley grinned. "Can you imagine Bracket looking over some South American broads through those thick glasses? Well, there's no time to talk, Styles. Pete and Louis, here, will take you down the firestairs to the basement." He glanced at the red exit light at the far end of the room. "Gunshots won't be very audible from down here. You can pray on the way." The second man had produced a gun from a shoulder holster.

"I think I'd rather take it here," Peter said.

"Sorry not to oblige," McCauley said. "March!"

Peter stood quiet still, holding the towel in his hand. He could hear voices from the lobby beyond. Gunshot would never go unnoticed here. The man with the gun took a step forward. Peter edged along the line of basins.

"Your two friends are the 'policemen' who tried to shoot up the Warfield from the roof last night?" he asked. "Tried to start a battle that would have made us look away from Larkspur?"

The man by the door grinned, but no one answered. Peter could guess what was coming. They wouldn't shoot him here. The two men would rush him and club him insensible and then drag him to the basement. He saw the man turn his gun around in his hand, just as Larch's man had done earlier that morning. It was to be used as a club.

Peter was not Sergeant Arthur Trotter, the little man with the Black Belt, but he wasn't going to be taken down too easily. He reached behind him and picked up a metal soap dish from one of the basins.

"No time to waste, Louis!" McCauley said.

Louis charged. Peter feinted to the left and dunked under the first swing with the gun butt. He came in close and raked Louis' face with the metal dish, and as Louis instinctively raised his hands toward his face Peter brought his knee up, savagely, into the man's groin. Then he turned and threw the soap dish with all his might at the long mirror over the basins. It shattered with an amazing amount of noise. McCauley and the man by the door were closing in. McCauley, the former bricklayer, was no soft touch. He and the man from the door fought without science or skill. The sheer weight of them, and the power in their fists was too much. Peter felt his head snap back from a solid clip to his jaw. As he staggered back he saw the door from the lobby open. There was a blur of faces as another blow to

180

the side of his head brought him down to his knees. He thought he saw McGraw. He thought he saw Ralph Cushing's white head. He heard a gunshot and the whine of a bullet. He lay where he was, his forehead pressed against the cool tile floor, waiting. There were loud, excited voices. Then someone took him firmly but gently by the arm and helped him to his feet.

"Today's punching bag," Maxvil said. He was smiling. "You hurt?"

"All over," Peter said. "But nothing critical, I guess." He looked past Maxvil and saw McCauley and his friends surrounded by McGraw and some of his men. "What the hell are you doing here, Greg?"

"Found out something I thought you ought to know," Maxvil said. "We gave Larch's office in Harlem a once-over. Too early to know much, but he had one thing in common with Larkspur. Same accountant. Edgar Bracket. I'm guessing his was the voice on your tape calling 'Tom.' And according to Mr. Cushing, 'Tom' is Theodore Osborn McCauley. You knew that too, I take it, or I wouldn't have found you lying on the floor in a public john."

Cushing was looking at Peter. "You've got a job to do before we start piecing this together, Styles."

Peter's head was throbbing. "Just a little piecing, sir, first," he said.

Devery was suddenly there, holding out Peter's coat and tie to him. "You okay, chum?"

"Would you believe you have to get kicked in the head to begin to see the shape of things?" Peter said. "Be a doll and see if you can find Andrew Callahan. He's out there in the lobby somewhere. Bring him to McGraw's office?"

"Will do," Devery said, handing Peter his coat.

"I'd like you and Lieutenant Maxvil in on this," Peter said. "Let's go."

They went out of the men's room, pushing their way through the excited crowd in the lobby to the little office. The minute the door closed Cushing had Peter by the arm. "The money is ready, Styles. You tell Conway that. If the hostages come out in one piece we can make a deal. We'll guarantee it in any way to satisfy him. Now that you've got McCauley and Larch, he should be satisfied."

"Right now I don't believe Larch was in on the Larkspur thing at all," Maxvil said. "But they had one thing in common: the same accountant—Edgar Bracket. It was Bracket who blew the ball game. He used Larch's phone to make a phone call to McCauley, and Crown's tape recorder picked it up. I told you, Peter, Larch couldn't function without someone in city government on his team. McCauley! And an accountant provided by McCauley. Larch heard a frightened Bracket talking to McCauley when your story broke. He knew his phone must be wired, and guessed the tapes had been turned over to you. He invaded your apartment in the hope of finding them. In walks Crown—and that was that."

"But why did Crown come to my place?"

"Bracket, talking again the day your story appeared, Crown heard it, knew what the 'plan' was and felt he had to stop it. He knew his phone tap would be discovered, couldn't reach Nathan Jones, came to you."

"And 'the plan'?"

"We'll know when the tapes turn up."

"If they turn up," Peter said.

"I have a strange hunch they may turn up at *Newsview*'s office in the mail. Crown was a careful man with evidence if not with his life."

"You've got to get on to Conway!" Cushing said.

"I want the whole story for him, Mr. Cushing. Just a minute or two." He turned as the office door opened and

Devery came in with Andrew Callahan in tow.

The lawyer looked as if he'd kept on with Bloody Marys after Peter had left him. His eyes were red and puffy.

"It's a wild world, Styles," he said. "Who'd have dreamed of McCauley?" He fumbled clumsily to light a cigarette. "First Girard and then McCauley; pillars of integrity, you'd have said."

"Like you," Peter said, his voice cold and hard.

Callahan's heavy lids lifted. "How's that?" he asked.

"There's one thing we're trying to clear up," Peter said. "The Swiss bank accounts. I understand Girard opened one for his wife."

Callahan nodded. "I recommended it. Tax purposes."

"And did you also recommend that he open one for himself?"

"Matter of fact I did."

"For tax purposes?"

"Yes."

"As Girard's lawyer, you had a power-of-attorney to act for him?"

"Yes, I did."

Peter's mouth was a thin, straight slit. "I tried to call you on the phone yesterday. Your office said you were out. I suddenly remember, now, in looking up your office number I noticed the address. It's in the Tompkins Building, right?"

"Yes."

"The same building in which Girard's offices are located?"

"Yes. But I don't understand what you're getting at, Styles."

"I am trying," Peter said, "to satisfy myself about Girard's death. You hinted to me a little while ago that Elaine and Gary Lehman were having an affair. I believe it. I believe Girard knew it at the very end. Did you hint at it

183

to him as you hinted at it to me?"

"No!"

"Because even if you did, Callahan, I simply can't believe that Girard would blow out his brains because he found his wife was cheating on him. Hurt, yes. Bitterly unhappy, yes. But Girard was a strong man, a man of character and accomplishment. What really happened? Did he find out that you, with your power-of-attorney, were siphoning off Larkspur funds into that Swiss bank account you'd opened for him?"

"No!" the corner of Callahan's mouth twitched, and he lifted a hand to hide it.

Peter turned toward Devery and the others. "I have to leave this to you, Frank, and you, Maxvil. There's Conway to deal with. But I suggest you ask Mr. Callahan how big a slice he got of the Larkspur graft from McCauley for handling that bank account."

"You must be out of your mind!" Callahan mumbled.

"I think Girard figured it out. I think he called Callahan down to his office sometime in the late afternoon of the day he died and asked some embarrassing questions. He then went up town to see his wife. Maybe he believed Callahan's hints about her and Gary, maybe he didn't. Then he went back to his office—to fight! Infidelity may have been hard to take, but the wrecking of his business reputation for honesty and integrity he couldn't let happen. Callahan had never left the office building, which is why the night man on the main floor never saw anyone come or go. Callahan went to Girard's office. They talked. I don't think Girard backed off. I think he faced Callahan with disaster, and I think Callahan, who knew that office as well as his own, took the gun out of Girard's desk drawer and killed him with it."

184

"The man is dreaming!" Callahan cried out, his voice shaken.

"Then he burned the documents. He knew better than anyone what had to be destroyed and where the material was. He cleared away all the dangerous evidence—and waited the rest of the night in his office so that no one would see him leave or knew he was there. I think, Maxvil, this man is a murderer, but it will be up to you to prove it."

"My pleasure," Maxvil said.

Callahan had slumped down into his chair, his face covered by his hands. He was crying.

Peter turned to the phone and dialed the number for Conway. Conway's cool voice answered after one ring.

"We've solved the problem on this end," Peter said. "We know who the key conspirators are. Three of them are under arrest—McCauley, Bracket, Andrew Callahan. We've also nailed Tony Larch. The Board is willing to replace the money in the Larkspur Fund. What do you offer in regard to the hostages?"

"I'm to take your word about the money?"

"What else do you want?"

There was a moment's hesitation. "Good enough," Conway said. "Have McGraw open up the Sixth Avenue end of the street. In five minutes from the time you hang up, six cars will come down the street to the theater. Before that we will release all the hostages but one—Elaine Summers. My men will then enter the cars with Miss Summers. We'll take her with us, and if we aren't followed, or tricked we'll release her when we're in the clear. If you double us, we'll chop her into very small pieces."

"Is she there? Can I talk to her?" Peter asked.

"Hold on."

Then Elaine's voice, calm, strong. "I'm willing to go with

185

them Peter. I think they'll do what they say."

"Listen to me, Elaine. You were right about your husband. Callahan killed him."

"Andrew!"

"And so that it isn't all happiness for you, Girard knew before he died that you had betrayed him."

"Oh, God! I hoped he hadn't. He didn't deserve to be hurt."

"Tell Conway to go!" Peter said.

He put down the phone and explained to Maxvil and Devery. Devery went out into the lobby to find McGraw. Peter walked over to the window. He felt exhausted. He watched the bleak face of the Warfield Theater, Elaine's name in dead light bulbs on the marquee. As far as he was concerned it was over. It was an old experience for him. Solving a crime never brought elation with it. Always after the fact; no techniques for preventing violence before it happened.

The phone was ringing. He ignored it because he was through. Suddenly he saw the inner lobby doors to the theater open and men and women came crowding out—the hostages. All but Elaine. And down from the far end of the street a parade of black cars appeared. If no one lost their heads Conway and his men—and Elaine—would be gone, to disappear into the indistinguishable mass that is a city.

Maxvil was tugging at his arm. "It's for you, Peter."

Peter went to the phone. Some last instructions from Conway, he imagined. An operators voice said: "Mr. Styles? I have a long distance call for you. Hold on."

Traced through the office or his message service, Peter thought. A cold chill ran along his spine. It would be Washington.

"Peter?" a faraway voice asked.

"This is Peter Styles," he said.

186

"Peter, darling!"

The room began to spin around him.

"Peter? Are you there? We crashed in the mountains— radio gone. We had to walk out—days of it. But I'm fine, Peter. They're flying me home. Sometime, late tomorrow—"

"Grace—darling!" He didn't recognize the sound of his own voice. "Oh my God! Grace!"

"Peter, the connection is so bad. Don't try to talk. Just be there!"

"I'll be there! Darling, will I be there!"

He put down the phone and stood there, frozen, a man in a trance.

"Here comes Conway with Mrs. Girard," someone said.

Peter didn't hear it. What he was hearing was Grace's voice speaking the words she'd once written to him. *All I want to be forever is your wife, your love, the other half of you who are the other half of me.*